100
SELECTED
POEMS

COLLECTABLE
EDITION

W. B. YEATS

CLASSICS

Published 2024

FiNGERPRINT! CLASSICS
Prakash Books

Fingerprint Publishing
@FingerprintP
@fingerprintpublishingbooks
www.fingerprintpublishing.com

ISBN: 978 93 8836 975 6

"Let us go forth, the tellers of tales, and seize whatever prey the heart long for, and have no fear. Everything exists, everything is true, and the earth is only a little dust under our feet."

—THE CELTIC TWILIGHT

One of the most influential figures of world literature, William Butler Yeats was born on June 13, 1865, at Sandymount in County Dublin, Ireland. He was a descendent of the Anglo-Irish Protestant minority and was the eldest son of John Butler Yeats, an Irish artist, and Susan Mary Pollexfen. The Yeats family moved to London two years after his birth. Yeats was educated at home along with his siblings in his early years. His mother narrated fairy tales and Irish folk tales to them, which largely inspired his early poetry. The legends and traditions kept him culturally rooted to his motherland throughout his life.

Between 1872 and 1874, Yeats spent a lot of time with his grandparents back in Sligo, Ireland. The culture and the magical countryside provided significant inspiration to the young poet. In 1876, the eleven-year-old Yeats joined his father in London, and the following year, enrolled at the Godolphin School, Hammersmith. An average student, he studied here for three years after which the family had to move back to Dublin. Here, he joined the Erasmus Smith High School in 1881.

With his father's studio close by, Yeats visited it often. He became acquainted with many artists and writers and began writing himself. In 1884, he joined the Dublin Metropolitan School of Art where he was introduced to the practice and study of the occult. This interest in the supernatural remained for life and is visible in his literary works. The following year, *The Island of Statues: An Arcadian Faery Tale in Two Acts* was serialized in the *Dublin University Review* between April and July. His first published work, it was never republished in his lifetime. In 1886, the pamphlet *Mosada: A Dramatic Poem* was published in the *Dublin University Review*.

The next year, Yeats returned to London with his family and visited Madame Helena Blavatsky, the renowned occultist and the co-founder of the Blavatsky Lodge, an English Theosophical society, which he joined towards the end of 1888. He also befriended William Morris, the British poet and social critic, who encouraged the young poet. Yeats contributed to the *Poems and Ballads of Young Ireland* (1888) and edited *Fairy and Folk Tales of Irish Peasantry*. He spent the Christmas of 1888 with Oscar Wilde, the Irish literary giant, who had a significant influence on him.

The first volume of his verse called *The Wanderings of Oisin and Other Poems* was published in 1889. A remarkable landmark in his literary career, it established his reputation as a poet. Apart from his epic poem *The Wanderings of Oisin*—based on the Fenian Cycle of Irish mythology—the collection included 'The Stolen Child', 'The Song of the Happy Shepherd', and 'The Indian to his Love' among other lyrical poems, which were collected under the heading *Crossways* in his later collections. These early lyrical verses were largely inspired from the works of P. B. Shelley, Edmund Spenser, and other pre-Raphaelite poets.

In the same year, on January 30, Yeats met Maud Gonne, an English heiress and Irish Nationalist, in London. Infatuated immediately by her beauty, Yeats fell madly in love with her. Unaware of her affair with Lucien Millevoye, Yeats proposed to her in 1891 but was spurned. Gonne remained his muse nonetheless and he addressed and dedicated several romantic verses to her including 'The Sorrow of Love' and 'When You Are Old'.

In the coming years, when Yeats proposed to her a couple of times but was turned down again, he told her that he was not happy without her. To this she replied: "Oh yes, you are, because you make beautiful poetry out of what you call your unhappiness, and are happy in that. Marriage would be such a dull affair. Poets should never marry. The world should thank me for not marrying you."

Yeats joined the Hermetic Order of the Golden Dawn, a magical order, in March 1890. The same year he founded the Rhymers' Club along with Ernest Rhys, T. W. Rolleston, and others. Rolleston and Yeats also co-founded the Irish Literary Society in London along with Charles Gavan Duffy in 1892. In June of the same year, Yeats established the National Literary Society in Dublin. In the later part of 1892, his second collection of poems, *The Countess Kathleen and Various Legends and Lyrics*, was published. It included his nationalistic play *The Countess Cathleen*, a poetic drama in blank verse inspired by Irish folklore and dedicated to Maud Gonne, and other shorter lyrics which were collected under *The Rose* in his later collections.

In 1893, *The Celtic Twilight*, a collection of essays and stories exploring the mysterious world of fairies, elves and other mythical beings was published. *The Land of Heart's Desire*, a fairy play, was produced at the Avenue Theatre in London the following year. Among the audience was Olivia Shakespear, a British playwright and novelist. Seated opposite each other at a literary dinner few days ago, they were not yet formally introduced. With their meeting began their friendship, which later turned into a love affair. 'The Lover Mourns for the Loss of Love' and 'The Travail of Passion' are among the poems he wrote for her.

Yeats met the esteemed Irish dramatist J. M. Synge in December of 1896. Synge had a lasting impression on the poet and many of his plays were produced at Abbey Theatre. In the last few years of the century, *Poems* (1895) and *The Wind Among the Reeds* (1899), collections of Yeats' early verses, were published. The poems in these collections were based on Irish legends and folklore. While most of them used symbols from everyday life and were rich with melodic beauty, several poems displayed his fascination with the supernatural through the use of occult symbolism. In 1899, Yeats, along with Lady Gregory, George Moore, and Edward Martyn, established the Irish Literary Theatre in Dublin. Their first production was *The Countess Cathleen*, performed in the Antient Concert Rooms, Dublin.

By the beginning of the twentieth century, Yeats had become a well-known literary figure in Dublin and London. He actively engaged in the management of Abbey Theatre in these initial years. He wrote several plays for the theatre, keeping in mind the simplicity and directness required in the dialogues for stage productions. Yeats met James Joyce in October 1902 at the National Library in Dublin. Contemporaries and critics, Yeats mentored Joyce, and in 1915, helped him obtain pension from the Royal Literary Fund.

In 1903, Yeats' sister, Elizabeth, first published *In the Seven Woods* with the subtitle 'Being Poems Chiefly of the Irish Heroic Age' at her Dun Emer Press, which later evolved into the Cuala Press and published works by Yeats, Rabindranath Tagore, Ezra Pound, and others. The collection included Yeats' long narrative poems—*The Old Age of Queen Maeve* and *Baile and Ailinn*, and the play *On Baile's Strand*, which was performed on the opening night of the Abbey Theatre in December 1904. In 1906 and 1907, *Poetical Works, I. Lyrical Poems* and *Poetical Works, II. Dramatic Poems* was published respectively. *The Collected Works in Verse and Prose* was published in eight volumes by Shakespeare Head Press between September and December 1908.

Yeats met Ezra Pound, the famous American poet, in 1909. Pound guided Yeats to write verses which were more modernistic than lyrical. The two poets spent a lot of time together during the period between 1913 and 1915 at the Stone

Cottage at Ashdown Forest, with Pound working as Yeats' secretary. Sometime around these years, Rabindranath Tagore had sailed to England from India with the English translations of his verses which later became the anthology *Gitanjali*. Yeats met Tagore and got to read his verses. He became an ardent proponent of Tagore's poems and also wrote an introduction for his anthology.

Having achieved a reputation internationally, Yeats began touring around the world giving lectures. *Poems: Second Series* (1910), *The Green Helmet and Other Poems* (1910), *Responsibilities: Poems and a Play* (1914), and *The Wild Swans at Coole* (1919) were his notable collections published in the first two decades of the twentieth century. The poems in these collections reflect a certain maturity and the developing realism of the period. The impact of the First World War (1914-1918) and the Irish troubles in 1916 also found way into the subject matter of Yeats' poetry.

Yeats declined the knighthood offered to him by the British Government in December 1915. The following year, the Easter Rising—a significant uprising initiated by the Irish Republicans against the British rule in Ireland—left a deep impact on him. Yeats penned down his reaction to the turn of events in his poem 'Easter 1916'. His support for the nationalistic cause gained strength and he decided to reside in Ireland.

On October 20, 1917, Yeats married Georgie Hyde-Lees, who was twenty-five then. They shared their interest in the occult and attempted automatic writing, a psychic phenomenon in which words are produced without being consciously written. They purportedly arise from a supernatural, spiritual, or a subconscious source. Yeats organized and studied the pages produced during the sleeping sessions and published his theories and beliefs about history and the individual in *A Vision* (1925). In November 1917, his collection *The Wild Swans at Coole*,

Other Verses and a Play in Verse was published. It was republished as *The Wild Swans at Coole* in 1919 without the play and with a dozen of additional poems.

The Irish War of Independence began in 1919 and continued till 1921. It was followed by the Irish Civil War (1922-1923). During this period, he published his collection of poems called *Michael Robartes and the Dancer* (February 1921). It contained some of his greatest poems like 'Easter 1916', 'Sixteen Dead Men', 'A Meditation in Time of War', and 'The Second Coming'. Inspired from the war scenes, these poems mirror the poet's troubled state of mind and his torn emotions. One of the best in the anthology, 'The Second Coming', written in blank verse, is an unrivalled expression of wartime fear and destructiveness and the brutality of man.

Yeats was nominated to the Irish Senate in December 1922. In November of the next year, the fifty-eight-year old Yeats became the first Irishman to be awarded the Nobel Prize in Literature. Yeats' artistic imagination was at its peak in the years that followed and he produced some of his best-known collections namely *The Tower* (1928), *The Winding Stairs and Other Poems* (1933), *Collected Poems* (1933), *Collected Plays* (1934), *A Full Moon in March* (1935), *New Poems* (1938), and *Last Poems and Two Plays* (1939). These works earned him the reputation of one of the most distinguished and influential poets of the twentieth century.

His poems 'Sailing to Byzantium', composed in 1926, and 'Byzantium', composed four years later, are not only famous but considered among the most remarkable poems of the world. They have for their theme an attempt to get away from the world of "sensual music", old age, and decay, to the immortal and eternal world with "unageing intellect" symbolized by Byzantium. The journey is a spiritual one. Yeats connected the real world with the world of the spirit through poetry.

He received an honorary doctorate from Oxford University in 1931. In the last few years of his life, despite his age and not keeping very well, Yeats remained quite active and enthusiastic. He not only wrote vigorously, but also had several romantic relationships. He edited a poetry anthology called the *Oxford Book of Modern Verse 1892–1935* in 1936. 'Under Ben Bulben', composed in August 1938, is considered to be his last poem. At seventy-four, Yeats breathed his last on January 28, 1939, in Menton, France, and was buried at Roquebrune-Cap-Martin.

Remembered and celebrated through his words and verses, Yeats was a gifted poet. His unparalleled imagination blended smoothly with his realistic vision helping him evolve from a romantic and symbolist to a realist and metaphysical poet. He used deftly devised symbols with allusive imagery and aided them with his knowledge and understanding of language and rhythm in his works, sticking mostly to the traditional verse forms. The Nobel Laureate's talent remains unsurpassed, and his timeless works continue to be admired and praised.

Contents

The Wanderings of Oisin

Published in *The Wanderings of Oisin and Other Poems* (1889)

Book I

S. Patrick

You who are bent, and bald, and blind,
With a heavy heart and a wandering mind,
Have known three centuries, poets sing,
Of dalliance with a demon thing.

Oisin

Sad to remember, sick with years,
The swift innumerable spears,
The horsemen with their floating hair,
And bowls of barley, honey, and wine,
Those merry couples dancing in tune,
And the white body that lay by mine;
But the tale, though words be lighter than air.
Must live to be old like the wandering moon.

Caoilte, and Conan*, and Finn were there,
When we followed a deer with our baying hounds.
With Bran, Sceolan, and Lomair,
And passing the Firbolgs'† burial-mounds,
Came to the cairn-heaped grassy hill
Where passionate Maeve is stony-still;
And found on the dove-grey edge of the sea
A pearl-pale, high-born lady, who rode
On a horse with bridle of findrinny‡;
And like a sunset were her lips,
A stormy sunset on doomed ships;
A citron colour gloomed in her hair,
But down to her feet white vesture flowed,
And with the glimmering crimson glowed
Of many a figured embroidery;
And it was bound with a pearl-pale shell
That wavered like the summer streams,
As her soft bosom rose and fell.

S. PATRICK
You are still wrecked among heathen dreams.

OISIN
'Why do you wind no horn?' she said.
'And every hero droop his head?
The hornless deer is not more sad
That many a peaceful moment had,

---

* The Thersites of the Fenian cycle.

† An early race who warred vainly upon the Fomorians, or Fomoroh, before becoming the Tuath De Danaan.

‡ A kind of red bronze.

More sleek than any granary mouse,
In his own leafy forest house
Among the waving fields of fern:
The hunting of heroes should be glad.'

'O pleasant woman,' answered Finn,
'We think on Oscar's pencilled urn,
And on the heroes lying slain
On Gabhra's raven-covered plain;
But where are your noble kith and kin,
And from what country do you ride?'

'My father and my mother are
Aengus and Edain, my own name
Niamh, and my country far
Beyond the tumbling of this tide.'

'What dream came with you that you came
Through bitter tide on foam-wet feet?
Did your companion wander away
From where the birds of Aengus wing?'

Thereon did she look haughty and sweet:
'I have not yet, war-weary king,
Been spoken of with any man;
Yet now I choose, for these four feet
Ran through the foam and ran to this
That I might have your son to kiss.'

'Were there no better than my son
That you through all that foam should run?'

'I loved no man, though kings besought,
Until the Danaan* poets brought
Rhyme that rhymed upon Oisin's name,
And now I am dizzy with the thought
Of all that wisdom and the fame
Of battles broken by his hands,
Of stories builded by his words
That are like coloured Asian birds
At evening in their rainless lands.'

O Patrick, by your brazen bell,
There was no limb of mine but fell
Into a desperate gulph of love!
'You only will I wed,' I cried,
'And I will make a thousand songs,
And set your name all names above,
And captives bound with leathern thongs
Shall kneel and praise you, one by one,
At evening in my western dun.'

'O Oisin, mount by me and ride
To shores by the wash of the tremulous tide,
Where men have heaped no burial-mounds,
And the days pass by like a wayward tune,
Where broken faith has never been known
And the blushes of first love never have flown;
And there I will give you a hundred hounds;

---

* Tuath De Danaan, meaning the Race of the Gods of Dana. Dana was the
mother of all ancient gods of Ireland. They were the powers of light and life
and warmth, and did battle with the Fomoroh, or powers of night and death
and cold. Robbed of offerings and honour, they have gradually dwindled in
the popular imagination until they have become the Faeries.

No mightier creatures bay at the moon;
And a hundred robes of murmuring silk,
And a hundred calves and a hundred sheep
Whose long wool whiter than sea-froth flows,
And a hundred spears and a hundred bows,
And oil and wine and honey and milk,
And always never-anxious sleep;
While a hundred youths, mighty of limb,
But knowing nor tumult nor hate nor strife,
And a hundred ladies, merry as birds,
Who when they dance to a fitful measure
Have a speed like the speed of the salmon herds,
Shall follow your horn and obey your whim,
And you shall know the Danaan leisure;
And Niamh be with you for a wife.'
Then she sighed gently, 'It grows late.
Music and love and sleep await,
Where I would be when the white moon climbs,
The red sun falls and the world grows dim.'

And then I mounted and she bound me
With her triumphing arms around me,
And whispering to herself enwound me;
But when the horse had felt my weight,
He shook himself and neighed three times:
Caoilte, Conan, and Finn came near,
And wept, and raised their lamenting hands,
And bid me stay, with many a tear;
But we rode out from the human lands.
In what far kingdom do you go,
Ah Fenians, with the shield and bow?
Or are you phantoms white as snow,

Whose lips had life's most prosperous glow?
O you, with whom in sloping valleys,
Or down the dewy forest alleys,
I chased at morn the flying deer,
With whom I hurled the hurrying spear,
And heard the foemen's bucklers rattle,
And broke the heaving ranks of battle!
And Bran, Sceolan, and Lomair,
Where are you with your long rough hair?
You go not where the red deer feeds,
Nor tear the foemen from their steeds.

S. PATRICK

Boast not, nor mourn with drooping head
Companions long accurst and dead,
And hounds for centuries dust and air.

OISIN

We galloped over the glossy sea:
I know not if days passed or hours,
And Niamh sang continually
Danaan songs, and their dewy showers
Of pensive laughter, unhuman sound,
Lulled weariness, and softly round
My human sorrow her white arms wound.
We galloped; now a hornless deer
Passed by us, chased by a phantom hound
All pearly white, save one red ear;
And now a lady rode like the wind
With an apple of gold in her tossing hand;
And a beautiful young man followed behind
With quenchless gaze and fluttering hair.

'Were these two born in the Danaan land,
Or have they breathed the mortal air?'

'Vex them no longer,' Niamh said,
And sighing bowed her gentle head,
And sighing laid the pearly tip
Of one long finger on my lip.

But now the moon like a white rose shone
In the pale west, and the sun's rim sank,
And clouds arrayed their rank on rank
About his fading crimson ball:
The floor of Almhuin's hosting hall
Was not more level than the sea,
As, full of loving fantasy,
And with low murmurs, we rode on,
Where many a trumpet-twisted shell
That in immortal silence sleeps
Dreaming of her own melting hues,
Her golds, her ambers, and her blues,
Pierced with soft light the shallowing deeps.
But now a wandering land breeze came
And a far sound of feathery quires;
It seemed to blow from the dying flame,
They seemed to sing in the smouldering fires.
The horse towards the music raced,
Neighing along the lifeless waste;
Like sooty fingers, many a tree
Rose ever out of the warm sea;
And they were trembling ceaselessly,
As though they all were beating time,
Upon the centre of the sun,

To that low laughing woodland rhyme.

And, now our wandering hours were done,
We cantered to the shore, and knew
The reason of the trembling trees:
Round every branch the song-birds flew,
Or clung thereon like swarming bees;
While round the shore a million stood
Like drops of frozen rainbow light,
And pondered in a soft vain mood
Upon their shadows in the tide,
And told the purple deeps their pride,
And murmured snatches of delight;
And on the shores were many boats
With bending sterns and bending bows,
And carven figures on their prows
Of bitterns, and fish-eating stoats,
And swans with their exultant throats:
And where the wood and waters meet
We tied the horse in a leafy clump,
And Niamh blew three merry notes
Out of a little silver trump;
And then an answering whispering flew
Over the bare and woody land,
A whisper of impetuous feet,
And ever nearer, nearer grew;
And from the woods rushed out a band
Of men and ladies, hand in hand,
And singing, singing all together;
Their brows were white as fragrant milk,
Their cloaks made out of yellow silk,
And trimmed with many a crimson feather;

And when they saw the cloak I wore
Was dim with mire of a mortal shore,
They fingered it and gazed on me
And laughed like murmurs of the sea;
But Niamh with a swift distress
Bid them away and hold their peace;
And when they heard her voice they ran
And knelt there, every girl and man,
And kissed, as they would never cease,
Her pearl-pale hand and the hem of her dress.
She bade them bring us to the hall
Where Aengus dreams, from sun to sun,
A Druid dream of the end of days
When the stars are to wane and the world
    be done.

They led us by long and shadowy ways
Where drops of dew in myriads fall,
And tangled creepers every hour
Blossom in some new crimson flower,
And once a sudden laughter sprang
From all their lips, and once they sang
Together, while the dark woods rang,
And made in all their distant parts,
With boom of bees in honey-marts,
A rumour of delighted hearts.
And once a lady by my side
Gave me a harp, and bid me sing,
And touch the laughing silver string;
But when I sang of human joy
A sorrow wrapped each merry face,
And, Patrick! by your beard, they wept,

Until one came, a tearful boy;
'A sadder creature never stept
Than this strange human bard,' he cried;
And caught the silver harp away,
And, weeping over the white strings, hurled
It down in a leaf-hid, hollow place
That kept dim waters from the sky;
And each one said, with a long, long sigh,
'O saddest harp in all the world,
Sleep there till the moon and the stars die!'

And now, still sad, we came to where
A beautiful young man dreamed within
A house of wattles, clay, and skin;
One hand upheld his beardless chin,
And one a sceptre flashing out
Wild flames of red and gold and blue,
Like to a merry wandering rout
Of dancers leaping in the air;
And men and ladies knelt them there
And showed their eyes with teardrops dim,
And with low murmurs prayed to him,
And kissed the sceptre with red lips,
And touched it with their finger-tips.

He held that flashing sceptre up.
'Joy drowns the twilight in the dew,
And fills with stars night's purple cup,
And wakes the sluggard seeds of corn,
And stirs the young kid's budding horn,
And makes the infant ferns unwrap,
And for the peewit paints his cap,

And rolls along the unwieldy sun,
And makes the little planets run:
And if joy were not on the earth,
There were an end of change and birth,
And Earth and Heaven and Hell would die,
And in some gloomy barrow lie
Folded like a frozen fly;
Then mock at Death and Time with glances
And wavering arms and wandering dances.

'Men's hearts of old were drops of flame
That from the saffron morning came,
Or drops of silver joy that fell
Out of the moon's pale twisted shell;
But now hearts cry that hearts are slaves,
And toss and turn in narrow caves;
But here there is nor law nor rule,
Nor have hands held a weary tool;
And here there is nor Change nor Death,
But only kind and merry breath,
For joy is God and God is joy.'
With one long glance on girl and boy
And the pale blossom of the moon,
He fell into a Druid swoon.

And in a wild and sudden dance
We mocked at Time and Fate and Chance
And swept out of the wattled hall
And came to where the dewdrops fall
Among the foamdrops of the sea,
And there we hushed the revelry;
And, gathering on our brows a frown,

Bent all our swaying bodies down,
And to the waves that glimmer by
That sloping green De Danaan sod
Sang, 'God is joy and joy is God,
And things that have grown sad are wicked,
And things that fear the dawn of the morrow
Or the grey wandering osprey Sorrow.'

We danced to where in the winding thicket
The damask roses, bloom on bloom,
Like crimson meteors hang in the gloom.
And bending over them softly said,
Bending over them in the dance,
With a swift and friendly glance
From dewy eyes: 'Upon the dead
Fall the leaves of other roses,
On the dead dim earth encloses:
But never, never on our graves,
Heaped beside the glimmering waves,
Shall fall the leaves of damask roses.
For neither Death nor Change comes near us,
And all listless hours fear us,
And we fear no dawning morrow,
Nor the grey wandering osprey Sorrow.'

The dance wound through the windless woods;
The ever-summered solitudes;
Until the tossing arms grew still
Upon the woody central hill;
And, gathered in a panting band,
We flung on high each waving hand,
And sang unto the starry broods.

In our raised eyes there flashed a glow
Of milky brightness to and fro
As thus our song arose: 'You stars,
Across your wandering ruby cars
Shake the loose reins: you slaves of God.
He rules you with an iron rod,
He holds you with an iron bond,
Each one woven to the other,
Each one woven to his brother
Like bubbles in a frozen pond;
But we in a lonely land abide
Unchainable as the dim tide,
With hearts that know nor law nor rule,
And hands that hold no wearisome tool,
Folded in love that fears no morrow,
Nor the grey wandering osprey Sorrow.'

O Patrick! for a hundred years
I chased upon that woody shore
The deer, the badger, and the boar.
O Patrick! for a hundred years
At evening on the glimmering sands,
Beside the piled-up hunting spears,
These now outworn and withered hands
Wrestled among the island bands.
O Patrick! for a hundred years
We went a-fishing in long boats
With bending sterns and bending bows,
And carven figures on their prows
Of bitterns and fish-eating stoats.
O Patrick! for a hundred years
The gentle Niamh was my wife;

But now two things devour my life;
The things that most of all I hate:
Fasting and prayers.

S. PATRICK
Tell On.

OISIN
Yes, yes,
For these were ancient Oisin's fate
Loosed long ago from Heaven's gate,
For his last days to lie in wait.
When one day by the tide I stood,
I found in that forgetfulness
Of dreamy foam a staff of wood
From some dead warrior's broken lance:
I turned it in my hands; the stains
Of war were on it, and I wept,
Remembering how the Fenians stept
Along the blood-bedabbled plains,
Equal to good or grievous chance:
Thereon young Niamh softly came
And caught my hands, but spake no word
Save only many times my name,
In murmurs, like a frighted bird.
We passed by woods, and lawns of clover,
And found the horse and bridled him,
For we knew well the old was over.
I heard one say, 'His eyes grow dim
With all the ancient sorrow of men';
And wrapped in dreams rode out again
With hoofs of the pale findrinny

Over the glimmering purple sea.
Under the golden evening light,
The immortals moved among the fountains
By rivers and the woods' old night;
Some danced like shadows on the mountains
Some wandered ever hand in hand;
Or sat in dreams on the pale strand,
Each forehead like an obscure star
Bent down above each hooked knee,
And sang, and with a dreamy gaze
Watched where the sun in a saffron blaze
Was slumbering half in the sea-ways;
And, as they sang, the painted birds
Kept time with their bright wings and feet;
Like drops of honey came their words,
But fainter than a young lamb's bleat.

'An old man stirs the fire to a blaze,
In the house of a child, of a friend, of a brother.
He has over-lingered his welcome; the days,
Grown desolate, whisper and sigh to each other;
He hears the storm in the chimney above,
And bends to the fire and shakes with the cold,
While his heart still dreams of battle and love,
And the cry of the hounds on the hills of old.
'But we are apart in the grassy places,
Where care cannot trouble the least of our days,
Or the softness of youth be gone from our faces,
Or love's first tenderness die in our gaze.
The hare grows old as she plays in the sun
And gazes around her with eyes of brightness;
Before the swift things that she dreamed of were done

She limps along in an aged whiteness;
A storm of birds in the Asian trees
Like tulips in the air a-winging,
And the gentle waves of the summer seas,
That raise their heads and wander singing,
Must murmur at last, "Unjust, unjust";
And "My speed is a weariness," falters the mouse,
And the kingfisher turns to a ball of dust,
And the roof falls in of his tunnelled house.
But the love-dew dims our eyes till the day
When God shall come from the sea with a sigh
And bid the stars drop down from the sky,
And the moon like a pale rose wither away.'

BOOK II

Now, man of croziers, shadows called our names
And then away, away, like whirling flames;
And now fled by, mist-covered, without sound,
The youth and lady and the deer and hound;
'Gaze no more on the phantoms,' Niamh said,
And kissed my eyes, and, swaying her bright head
And her bright body, sang of faery and man
Before God was or my old line began;
Wars shadowy, vast, exultant; faeries of old
Who wedded men with rings of Druid gold;
And how those lovers never turn their eyes
Upon the life that fades and flickers and dies,
Yet love and kiss on dim shores far away
Rolled round with music of the sighing spray:
Yet sang no more as when, like a brown bee
That has drunk full, she crossed the misty sea

With me in her white arms a hundred years
Before this day; for now the fall of tears
Troubled her song.
                            I do not know if days
Or hours passed by, yet hold the morning rays
Shone many times among the glimmering flowers
Woven into her hair, before dark towers
Rose in the darkness, and the white surf gleamed
About them; and the horse of Faery screamed
And shivered, knowing the Isle of Many Fears,
Nor ceased until white Niamh stroked his ears
And named him by sweet names.

                                    A foaming tide
Whitened afar with surge, fan-formed and wide,
Burst from a great door marred by many a blow
From mace and sword and pole-axe, long ago
When gods and giants warred. We rode between
The seaweed-covered pillars; and the green
And surging phosphorus alone gave light
On our dark pathway, till a countless flight
Of moonlit steps glimmered; and left and right
Dark statues glimmered over the pale tide
Upon dark thrones. Between the lids of one
The imaged meteors had flashed and run
And had disported in the stilly jet,
And the fixed stars had dawned and shone and set,
Since God made Time and Death and Sleep: the other
Stretched his long arm to where, a misty smother,
The stream churned, churned, and churned—his
        lips apart,
As though he told his never-slumbering heart

Of every foamdrop on its misty way.
Tying the horse to his vast foot that lay
Half in the unvesselled sea, we climbed the stair
And climbed so long, I thought the last steps were
Hung from the morning star; when these mild words
Fanned the delighted air like wings of birds:
'My brothers spring out of their beds at morn,
A-murmur like young partridge: with loud horn
They chase the noontide deer;
And when the dew-drowned stars hang in the air
Look to long fishing-lines, or point and pare
An ashen hunting spear.
O sigh, O fluttering sigh, be kind to me;
Flutter along the froth lips of the sea,
And shores, the froth lips wet:
And stay a little while, and bid them weep:
Ah, touch their blue-veined eyelids if they sleep,
And shake their coverlet.
When you have told how I weep endlessly,
Flutter along the froth lips of the sea
And home to me again,
And in the shadow of my hair lie hid,
And tell me that you found a man unbid,
The saddest of all men.'

A lady with soft eyes like funeral tapers,
And face that seemed wrought out of moonlit
    vapours,
And a sad mouth, that fear made tremulous
As any ruddy moth, looked down on us;
And she with a wave-rusted chain was tied
To two old eagles, full of ancient pride,

That with dim eyeballs stood on either side.
Few feathers were on their dishevelled wings,
For their dim minds were with the ancient things.

'I bring deliverance,' pearl-pale Niamh said.

'Neither the living, nor the unlabouring dead,
Nor the high gods who never lived, may fight
My enemy and hope; demons for fright
Jabber and scream about him in the night;
For he is strong and crafty as the seas
That sprang under the Seven Hazel Trees,[*]
And I must needs endure and hate and weep,
Until the gods and demons drop asleep,
Hearing Aedh[†] touch the mournful strings of gold.'

'Is he so dreadful?'
                'Be not over-bold,
But fly while still you may.'
                     And thereon I:
'This demon shall be battered till he die,
And his loose bulk be thrown in the loud tide.'

'Flee from him,' pearl-pale Niamh weeping cried,
'For all men flee the demons'; but moved not
My angry king remembering soul one jot.
There was no mightier soul of Heber's line;

---

[*] There was once a well overshadowed by seven sacred hazel trees, in the midst of Ireland. A certain lady plucked their fruit, and seven rivers arose out of the well and swept her away. In my poems, this well is the source of all waters of this world, which are therefore sevenfold.

[†] A Celtic God of death.

Now it is old and mouse-like. For a sign
I burst the chain: still earless, nerveless, blind,
Wrapped in the things of the unhuman mind,
In some dim memory or ancient mood,
Still earless, nerveless, blind, the eagles stood.

And then we climbed the stair to a high door;
A hundred horsemen on the basalt floor
Beneath had paced content: we held our way
And stood within: clothed in a misty ray
I saw a foam-white seagull drift and float
Under the roof, and with a straining throat
Shouted, and hailed him: he hung there a star,
For no man's cry shall ever mount so far;
Not even your God could have thrown down that
        hall;
Stabling His unloosed lightnings in their stall,
He had sat down and sighed with cumbered heart,
As though His hour were come.

                    We sought the part
That was most distant from the door; green slime
Made the way slippery, and time on time
Showed prints of sea-born scales, while down
        through it
The captive's journeys to and fro were writ
Like a small river, and where feet touched, came
A momentary gleam of phosphorus flame.
Under the deepest shadows of the hall
That woman found a ring hung on the wall,
And in the ring a torch, and with its flare
Making a world about her in the air,

Passed under the dim doorway, out of sight,
And came again, holding a second light
Burning between her fingers, and in mine
Laid it and sighed: I held a sword whose shine
No centuries could dim, and a word ran
Thereon in Ogham letters, 'Manannan';
That sea-god's name, who in a deep content
Sprang dripping, and, with captive demons sent
Out of the sevenfold seas, built the dark hall
Rooted in foam and clouds, and cried to all
The mightier masters of a mightier race;
And at his cry there came no milk-pale face
Under a crown of thorns and dark with blood,
But only exultant faces.

                  Niamh stood
With bowed head, trembling when the white
    blade shone,
But she whose hours of tenderness were gone
Had neither hope nor fear. I bade them hide
Under the shadows till the tumults died
Of the loud-crashing and earth-shaking fight,
Lest they should look upon some dreadful sight;
And thrust the torch between the slimy flags.
A dome made out of endless carven jags,
Where shadowy face flowed into shadowy face,
Looked down on me; and in the self-same place
I waited hour by hour, and the high dome,
Windowless, pillarless, multitudinous home
Of faces, waited; and the leisured gaze
Was loaded with the memory of days
Buried and mighty. When through the great door
The dawn came in, and glimmered on the floor

With a pale light, I journeyed round the hall
And found a door deep sunken in the wall,
The least of doors; beyond on a dim plain
A little runnel made a bubbling strain,
And on the runnel's stony and bare edge
A dusky demon dry as a withered sedge
Swayed, crooning to himself an unknown tongue:
In a sad revelry he sang and swung
Bacchant and mournful, passing to and fro
His hand along the runnel's side, as though
The flowers still grew there: far on the sea's waste
Shaking and waving, vapour vapour chased,
While high frail cloudlets, fed with a green light,
Like drifts of leaves, immovable and bright,
Hung in the passionate dawn. He slowly turned:
A demon's leisure: eyes, first white, now burned
Like wings of kingfishers; and he arose
Barking. We trampled up and down with blows
Of sword and brazen battle-axe, while day
Gave to high noon and noon to night gave way;
And when he knew the sword of Manannan
Amid the shades of night, he changed and ran
Through many shapes; I lunged at the smooth
    throat
Of a great eel; it changed, and I but smote
A fir-tree roaring in its leafless top;
And thereupon I drew the livid chop
Of a drowned dripping body to my breast;
Horror from horror grew; but when the west
Had surged up in a plumy fire, I drave
Through heart and spine; and cast him in the wave
Lest Niamh shudder.

        Full of hope and dread
Those two came carrying wine and meat and bread,
And healed my wounds with unguents out of
    flowers
That feed white moths by some De Danaan shrine;
Then in that hall, lit by the dim sea-shine,
We lay on skins of otters, and drank wine,
Brewed by the sea-gods, from huge cups that lay
Upon the lips of sea-gods in their day;
And then on heaped-up skins of otters slept.
And when the sun once more in saffron stept,
Rolling his flagrant wheel out of the deep,
We sang the loves and angers without sleep,
And all the exultant labours of the strong.
But now the lying clerics murder song
With barren words and flatteries of the weak.
In what land do the powerless turn the beak
Of ravening Sorrow, or the hand of Wrath?
For all your croziers, they have left the path
And wander in the storms and clinging snows,
Hopeless for ever: ancient Oisin knows,
For he is weak and poor and blind, and lies
On the anvil of the world.

        S. Patrick
        Be still: the skies
Are choked with thunder, lightning, and fierce
    wind,
For God has heard, and speaks His angry mind;
Go cast your body on the stones and pray,
For He has wrought midnight and dawn and day.

OISIN

Saint, do you weep? I hear amid the thunder
The Fenian horses; armour torn asunder;
Laughter and cries. The armies clash and shock,
And now the daylight-darkening ravens flock.
Cease, cease, O mournful, laughing Fenian horn!

We feasted for three days. On the fourth morn
I found, dropping sea-foam on the wide stair,
And hung with slime, and whispering in his hair,
That demon dull and unsubduable;
And once more to a day-long battle fell,
And at the sundown threw him in the surge,
To lie until the fourth morn saw emerge
His new-healed shape; and for a hundred years
So warred, so feasted, with nor dreams nor fears,
Nor languor nor fatigue: an endless feast,
An endless war.

       The hundred years had ceased;
I stood upon the stair: the surges bore
A beech-bough to me, and my heart grew sore,
Remembering how I had stood by white-haired
    Finn
Under a beech at Almhuin and heard the thin
Outcry of bats.

       And then young Niamh came
Holding that horse, and sadly called my name;
I mounted, and we passed over the lone
And drifting greyness, while this monotone,
Surly and distant, mixed inseparably

Into the clangour of the wind and sea.
'I hear my soul drop
And Manannan's dark tower, stone after stone.
Gather sea-slime and fall the seaward way,
And the moon goad the waters night and day,
That all be overthrown.

'But till the moon has taken all, I wage
War on the mightiest men under the skies,
And they have fallen or fled, age after age.
Light is man's love, and lighter is man's rage;
His purpose drifts and dies.'

And then lost Niamh murmured, 'Love, we go
To the Island of Forgetfulness, for lo!
The Islands of Dancing and of Victories
Are empty of all power.'

    'And which of these
Is the Island of Content?'

    'None know,' she said;
And on my bosom laid her weeping head.

BOOK III

Fled foam underneath us, and round us, a
  wandering and milky smoke,
High as the saddle-girth, covering away from our
  glances the tide;
And those that fled, and that followed, from the
  foam-pale distance broke;

The immortal desire of immortals we saw in their
    faces, and sighed.
I mused on the chase with the Fenians, and Bran,
    Sceolan, Lomair,
And never a song sang Niamh, and over my
    finger-tips
Came now the sliding of tears and sweeping of
    mist-cold hair,
And now the warmth of sighs, and after the
    quiver of lips.

Were we days long or hours long in riding, when,
    rolled in a grisly peace,
An isle lay level before us, with dripping hazel
    and oak?
And we stood on a sea's edge we saw not; for
    whiter than new-washed fleece
Fled foam underneath us, and round us, a
    wandering and milky smoke.

And we rode on the plains of the sea's edge; the
    sea's edge barren and grey,
Grey sand on the green of the grasses and over
    the dripping trees,
Dripping and doubling landward, as though they
    would hasten away,
Like an army of old men longing for rest from the
    moan of the seas.

But the trees grew taller and closer, immense in
    their wrinkling bark;

Dropping; a murmurous dropping; old silence
    and that one sound;
For no live creatures lived there, no weasels
    moved in the dark:
Long sighs arose in our spirits, beneath us
    bubbled the ground.

And the ears of the horse went sinking away in
    the hollow night,
For, as drift from a sailor slow drowning the
    gleams of the world and the sun,
Ceased on our hands and our faces, on hazel and
    oak leaf, the light,
And the stars were blotted above us, and the
    whole of the world was one.

Till the horse gave a whinny; for, cumbrous with
    stems of the hazel and oak,
A valley flowed down from his hoofs, and there in
    the long grass lay,
Under the starlight and shadow, a monstrous
    slumbering folk,
Their naked and gleaming bodies poured out and
    heaped in the way.

And by them were arrow and war-axe, arrow and
    shield and blade;
And dew-blanched horns, in whose hollow a child
    of three years old
Could sleep on a couch of rushes, and all
    inwrought and inlaid,

And more comely than man can make them with
    bronze and silver and gold.

And each of the huge white creatures was huger
    than fourscore men;
The tops of their ears were feathered, their hands
    were the claws of birds,
And, shaking the plumes of the grasses and the
    leaves of the mural glen,
The breathing came from those bodies, long
    warless, grown whiter than curds.

The wood was so Spacious above them, that He
    who has stars for His flocks
Could fondle the leaves with His fingers, nor go
    from His dew-cumbered skies;
So long were they sleeping, the owls had builded
    their nests in their locks,
Filling the fibrous dimness with long generations
    of eyes.

And over the limbs and the valley the slow owls
    wandered and came,
Now in a place of star-fire, and now in a shadow-
    place wide;
And the chief of the huge white creatures, his
    knees in the soft star-flame,
Lay loose in a place of shadow: we drew the reins
    by his side.

Golden the nails of his bird-claws, flung loosely
    along the dim ground;

In one was a branch soft-shining, with bells more
    many than sighs,
In midst of an old man's bosom; owls ruffling and
    pacing around,
Sidled their bodies against him, filling the shade
    with their eyes.

And my gaze was thronged with the sleepers; no,
    not since the world began,
In realms where the handsome were many, nor in
    glamours by demons flung,
Have faces alive with such beauty been known to
    the salt eye of man,
Yet weary with passions that faded when the
    sevenfold seas were young.

And I gazed on the bell-branch*, sleep's forebear,
    far sung by the Sennachies.
I saw how those slumberers, grown weary, there
    camping in grasses deep,
Of wars with the wide world and pacing the
    shores of the wandering seas,
Laid hands on the bell-branch and swayed it, and
    fed of unhuman sleep.

Snatching the horn of Niamh, I blew a long
    lingering note.
Came sound from those monstrous sleepers, a
    sound like the stirring of flies.

---

* A legendary branch whose shaking casts all men into a sleep.

He, shaking the fold of his lips, and heaving the
    pillar of his throat,
Watched me with mournful wonder out of the
    wells of his eyes.

I cried, 'Come out of the shadow, king of the nails
    of gold!
And tell of your goodly household and the goodly
    works of your hands,
That we may muse in the starlight and talk of the
    battles of old;
Your questioner, Oisin, is worthy, he comes from
    the Fenian lands.'

Half open his eyes were, and held me, dull with
    the smoke of their dreams;
His lips moved slowly in answer, no answer out of
    them came;
Then he swayed in his fingers the bell-branch,
    slow dropping a sound in faint streams
Softer than snow-flakes in April and piercing the
    marrow like flame.

Wrapt in the wave of that music, with weariness
    more than of earth,
The moil of my centuries filled me; and gone like
    a sea-covered stone
Were the memories of the whole of my sorrow
    and the memories of the whole of my mirth,
And a softness came from the starlight and filled
    me full to the bone.

In the roots of the grasses, the sorrels, I laid my
  body as low;
And the pearl-pale Niamh lay by me, her brow on
  the midst of my breast;
And the horse was gone in the distance, and years
  after years 'gan flow;
Square leaves of the ivy moved over us, binding
  us down to our rest.

And, man of the many white croziers, a century
  there I forgot
How the fetlocks drip blood in the battle, when
  the fallen on fallen lie rolled;
How the falconer follows the falcon in the weeds
  of the heron's plot,
And the name of the demon whose hammer made
  Conchubar's* sword-blade of old.

And, man of the many white croziers, a century
  there I forgot
That the spear-shaft is made out of ashwood, the
  shield out of osier and hide;
How the hammers spring on the anvil, on the
  spearhead's burning spot;
How the slow, blue-eyed oxen of Finn low sadly at
  evening tide.
But in dreams, mild man of the croziers, driving
  the dust with their throngs,
Moved round me, of seamen or landsmen, all who
  are winter tales;

---

* Conchubar was King of all Ireland in the time of the Red Branch Kings.

Came by me the kings of the Red Branch, with
    roaring of laughter and songs,
Or moved as they moved once, love-making or
    piercing the tempest with sails.

Came Blanid*, Mac Nessa, tall Fergus who
    feastward of old time slunk,
Cook Barach†, the traitor; and warward, the spittle
    on his beard never dry,
Dark Balor‡, as old as a forest, car-borne, his
    mighty head sunk
Helpless, men lifting the lids of his weary and
    death-making eye.
And by me, in soft red raiment, the Fenians
    moved in loud streams,
And Grania, walking and smiling, sewed with her
    needle of bone.
So lived I and lived not, so wrought I and wrought
    not, with creatures of dreams,
In a long iron sleep, as a fish in the water goes
    dumb as a stone.

At times our slumber was lightened. When the
    sun was on silver or gold;

---

* The heroine of a beautiful and sad story told by Keating.
† Barach enticed Fergus away to a feast, that the sons of Usna might be killed in his absence. Fergus had made an oath never to refuse a feast from him, and so was compelled to go, though all unwillingly.
‡ The Irish Chimaera, the leader of the hosts of darkness at the great battle of good and evil, life and death, light and darkness, which was fought out on the strands of Moytura, near Sligo.

When brushed with the wings of the owls, in the
    dimness they love going by;
When a glow-worm was green on a grass-leaf,
    lured from his lair in the mould;
Half wakening, we lifted our eyelids, and gazed
    on the grass with a sigh.

So watched I when, man of the croziers, at the
    heel of a century fell,
Weak, in the midst of the meadow, from his miles
    in the midst of the air,
A starling like them that forgathered 'neath a
    moon waking white as a shell
When the Fenians made foray at morning with
    Bran, Sceolan, Lomair.

I awoke: the strange horse without summons out
    of the distance ran,
Thrusting his nose to my shoulder; he knew in his
    bosom deep
That once more moved in my bosom the ancient
    sadness of man,
And that I would leave the immortals, their
    dimness, their dews dropping sleep.

O, had you seen beautiful Niamh grow white as
    the waters are white,
Lord of the croziers, you even had lifted your
    hands and wept:
But, the bird in my fingers, I mounted, remembering
    alone that delight

Of twilight and slumber were gone, and that
    hoofs impatiently stept.

I cried, 'O Niamh! O white one! if only a twelve-
    houred day,
I must gaze on the beard of Finn, and move
    where the old men and young
In the Fenians' dwellings of wattle lean on the
    chessboards and play,
Ah, sweet to me now were even bald Conan's
    slanderous tongue!

'Like me were some galley forsaken far off in
    Meridian isle,
Remembering its long-oared companions, sails
    turning to threadbare rags;
No more to crawl on the seas with long oars mile
    after mile,
But to be amid shooting of flies and flowering of
    rushes and flags.'

Their motionless eyeballs of spirits grown mild
    with mysterious thought,
Watched her those seamless faces from the
    valley's glimmering girth;
As she murmured, 'O wandering Oisin, the
    strength of the bell-branch is naught,
For there moves alive in your fingers the
    fluttering sadness of earth.

'Then go through the lands in the saddle and see
    what the mortals do,

And softly come to your Niamh over the tops of
    the tide;
But weep for your Niamh, O Oisin, weep; for if
    only your shoe
Brush lightly as haymouse earth's pebbles, you
    will come no more to my side.

'O flaming lion of the world, O when will you
    turn to your rest?'
I saw from a distant saddle; from the earth she
    made her moan:
'I would die like a small withered leaf in the
    autumn, for breast unto breast
We shall mingle no more, nor our gazes empty
    their sweetness lone

'In the isles of the farthest seas where only the
    spirits come.
Were the winds less soft than the breath of a
    pigeon who sleeps on her nest,
Nor lost in the star-fires and odours the sound of
    the sea's vague drum?
O flaming lion of the world, O when will you
    turn to your rest?'

The wailing grew distant; I rode by the woods of
    the wrinkling bark,
Where ever is murmurous dropping, old silence
    and that one sound;
For no live creatures live there, no weasels move
    in the dark:

In a reverie forgetful of all things, over the
    bubbling ground.

And I rode by the plains of the sea's edge, where
    all is barren and grey,
Grey sands on the green of the grasses and over
    the dripping trees,
Dripping and doubling landward, as though they
    would hasten away,
Like an army of old men longing for rest from the
    moan of the seas.

And the winds made the sands on the sea's edge
    turning and turning go,
As my mind made the names of the Fenians. Far
    from the hazel and oak,
I rode away on the surges, where, high as the
    saddle-bow,
Fled foam underneath me, and round me, a
    wandering and milky smoke.

Long fled the foam-flakes around me, the winds
    fled out of the vast,
Snatching the bird in secret; nor knew I,
    embosomed apart,
When they froze the cloth on my body like
    armour riveted fast,
For Remembrance, lifting her leanness, keened in
    the gates of my heart.

Till, fattening the winds of the morning, an odour
    of new-mown hay

Came, and my forehead fell low, and my tears like
    berries fell down;
Later a sound came, half lost in the sound of a
    shore far away,
From the great grass-barnacle calling, and later
    the shore-weeds brown.

If I were as I once was, the strong hoofs crushing
    the sand and the shells,
Coming out of the sea as the dawn comes, a
    chaunt of love on my lips,
Not coughing, my head on my knees, and praying,
    and wroth with the bells,
I would leave no saint's head on his body from
    Rachlin to Bera of ships.

Making way from the kindling surges, I rode on a
    bridle-path
Much wondering to see upon all hands, of wattles
    and woodwork made,
Your bell-mounted churches, and guardless the
    sacred cairn and the rath,
And a small and a feeble populace stooping with
    mattock and spade,

Or weeding or ploughing with faces a-shining
    with much-toil wet;
While in this place and that place, with bodies
    unglorious, their chieftains stood,
Awaiting in patience the straw-death, croziered
    one, caught in your net:

Went the laughter of scorn from my mouth like
    the roaring of wind in a wood.

And before I went by them so huge and so speedy
    with eyes so bright,
Came after the hard gaze of youth, or an old man
    lifted his head:
And I rode and I rode, and I cried out, 'The
    Fenians hunt wolves in the night,
So sleep thee by daytime.' A voice cried, 'The
    Fenians a long time are dead.'

A whitebeard stood hushed on the pathway, the
    flesh of his face as dried grass,
And in folds round his eyes and his mouth, he sad
    as a child without milk—
And the dreams of the islands were gone, and I
    knew how men sorrow and pass,
And their hound, and their horse, and their love,
    and their eyes that glimmer like silk.

And wrapping my face in my hair, I murmured,
    'In old age they ceased';
And my tears were larger than berries, and I
    murmured, 'Where white clouds lie spread
On Crevroe or broad Knockfefin, with many of
    old they feast
On the floors of the gods.' He cried, 'No, the
    gods a long time are dead.'

And lonely and longing for Niamh, I shivered and
    turned me about,

The heart in me longing to leap like a grasshopper
    into her heart;
I turned and rode to the westward, and followed
    the sea's old shout
Till I saw where Maeve lies sleeping till starlight
    and midnight part.

And there at the foot of the mountain, two
    carried a sack full of sand,
They bore it with staggering and sweating, but fell
    with their burden at length.
Leaning down from the gem-studded saddle, I
    flung it five yards with my hand,
With a sob for men waxing so weakly, a sob for
    the Fenians' old strength.

The rest you have heard of, O croziered man;
    how, when divided the girth,
I fell on the path, and the horse went away like a
    summer fly;
And my years three hundred fell on me, and I
    rose, and walked on the earth,
A creeping old man, full of sleep, with the spittle
    on his beard never dry.

How the men of the sand-sack showed me a
    church with its belfry in air;
Sorry place, where for swing of the war-axe in my
    dim eyes the crozier gleams;
What place have Caoilte and Conan, and Bran,
    Sceolan, Lomair?

Speak, you too are old with your memories, an old
    man surrounded with dreams.

S. PATRICK

Where the flesh of the footsole clingeth on the
    burning stones is their place;
Where the demons whip them with wires on the
    burning stones of wide Hell,
Watching the blessed ones move far off, and the
    smile on God's face,
Between them a gateway of brass, and the howl of
    the angels who fell.

OISIN

Put the staff in my hands; for I go to the Fenians,
    O cleric, to chaunt
The war-songs that roused them of old; they will
    rise, making clouds with their breath,
Innumerable, singing, exultant; the clay
    underneath them shall pant,
And demons be broken in pieces, and trampled
    beneath them in death.

And demons afraid in their darkness; deep horror
    of eyes and of wings,
Afraid, their ears on the earth laid, shall listen and
    rise up and weep;
Hearing the shaking of shields and the quiver of
    stretched bowstrings,
Hearing Hell loud with a murmur, as shouting
    and mocking we sweep.

We will tear out the flaming stones, and batter the
    gateway of brass
And enter, and none sayeth 'No' when there
    enters the strongly armed guest;
Make clean as a broom cleans, and march on as
    oxen move over young grass;
Then feast, making converse of wars, and of old
    wounds, and turn to our rest.

S. Patrick

On the flaming stones, without refuge, the limbs
    of the Fenians are tost;
None war on the masters of Hell, who could
    break up the world in their rage;
But kneel and wear out the flags and pray for your
    soul that is lost
Through the demon love of its youth and its
    godless and passionate age.

Oisin

Ah me! to be shaken with coughing and broken
    with old age and pain,
Without laughter, a show unto children, alone
    with remembrance and fear;
All emptied of purple hours as a beggar's cloak in
    the rain,
As a hay-cock out on the flood, or a wolf sucked
    under a weir.

It were sad to gaze on the blessed and no man I
    loved of old there;

I throw down the chain of small stones! when life
  in my body has ceased,
I will go to Caoilte, and Conan, and Bran,
  Sceolan, Lomair,
And dwell in the house of the Fenians, be they in
  flames or at feast.

The Song of the Happy Shepherd

Composed 1885
Published in *The Wanderings of Oisin and Other Poems* (1889)
Collected under *Crossways* in his later collections

The woods of Arcady are dead,
And over is their antique joy;
Of old the world on dreaming fed;
Grey Truth is now her painted toy;
Yet still she turns her restless head:
But O, sick children of the world,
Of all the many changing things
In dreary dancing past us whirled,
To the cracked tune that Chronos sings,
Words alone are certain good.
Where are now the warring kings,
Word be-mockers?—By the Rood,
Where are now the warring kings?
An idle word is now their glory,
By the stammering schoolboy said,
Reading some entangled story:
The kings of the old time are dead;
The wandering earth herself may be

Only a sudden flaming word,
In clanging space a moment heard,
Troubling the endless reverie.

Then nowise worship dusty deeds,
Nor seek, for this is also sooth,
To hunger fiercely after truth,
Lest all thy toiling only breeds
New dreams, new dreams; there is no truth
Saving in thine own heart. Seek, then,
No learning from the starry men,
Who follow with the optic glass
The whirling ways of stars that pass—
Seek, then, for this is also sooth,
No word of theirs—the cold star-bane
Has cloven and rent their hearts in twain,
And dead is all their human truth.
Go gather by the humming sea
Some twisted, echo-harbouring shell,
And to its lips thy story tell,
And they thy comforters will be,
Rewording in melodious guile
Thy fretful words a little while,
Till they shall singing fade in ruth
And die a pearly brotherhood;
For words alone are certain good:
Sing, then, for this is also sooth.

I must be gone: there is a grave
Where daffodil and lily wave,
And I would please the hapless faun,
Buried under the sleepy ground,

With mirthful songs before the dawn.
His shouting days with mirth were crowned;
And still I dream he treads the lawn,
Walking ghostly in the dew,
Pierced by my glad singing through,
My songs of old earth's dreamy youth:
But ah! she dreams not now; dream thou!
For fair are poppies on the brow:
Dream, dream, for this is also sooth.

The Sad Shepherd

Composed 1885
Published in *The Wanderings of Oisin and Other Poems* (1889)
Collected under *Crossways* in his later collections

There was a man whom Sorrow named his Friend,
And he, of his high comrade Sorrow dreaming,
Went walking with slow steps along the gleaming
And humming sands, where windy surges wend:
And he called loudly to the stars to bend
From their pale thrones and comfort him, but they
Among themselves laugh on and sing alway:
And then the man whom Sorrow named his friend
Cried out, *Dim sea, hear my most piteous story!*
The sea swept on and cried her old cry still,
Rolling along in dreams from hill to hill.
He fled the persecution of her glory
And, in a far-off, gentle valley stopping,
Cried all his story to the dewdrops glistening.
But naught they heard, for they are always listening,
The dewdrops, for the sound of their own dropping.
And then the man whom Sorrow named his friend
Sought once again the shore, and found a shell,
And thought, *I will my heavy story tell*

Till my own words, re-echoing, shall send
Their sadness through a hollow, pearly heart;
And my own tale again for me shall sing,
And my own whispering words be comforting,
And lo! my ancient burden may depart.
Then he sang softly nigh the pearly rim;
But the sad dweller by the sea-ways lone
Changed all he sang to inarticulate moan
Among her wildering whirls, forgetting him.

The Cloak, the Boat, and the Shoes

Published in *The Wanderings of Oisin and Other Poems* (1889)
Collected under *Crossways* in his later collections

'What do you make so fair and bright?'

'I make the cloak of Sorrow:
O lovely to see in all men's sight
Shall be the cloak of Sorrow,
In all men's sight.'

'What do you build with sails for flight?'

'I build a boat for Sorrow:
O swift on the seas all day and night
Saileth the rover Sorrow,
All day and night.'

'What do you weave with wool so white?'

'I weave the shoes of Sorrow:
Soundless shall be the footfall light
In all men's ears of Sorrow,
Sudden and light.'

The Indian Upon God

Published in *The Wanderings of Oisin and Other Poems* (1889)
Collected under *Crossways* in his later collections

I passed along the water's edge below the humid
    trees,
My spirit rocked in evening light, the rushes
    round my knees,
My spirit rocked in sleep and sighs; and saw the
    moorfowl pace
All dripping on a grassy slope, and saw them
    cease to chase
Each other round in circles, and heard the eldest
    speak:
Who holds the world between His bill and made us strong
    or weak
Is an undying moorfowl, and He lives beyond the sky.
The rains are from His dripping wing, the moonbeams
    from his eye.
I passed a little further on and heard a lotus talk:
Who made the world and ruleth it, He hangeth on a stalk,
For I am in His image made, and all this tinkling tide
Is but a sliding drop of rain between His petals wide.

A little way within the gloom a roebuck raised his
    eyes

Brimful of starlight, and he said: *The Stamper of the
    Skies,*

He is a gentle roebuck; for how else, I pray, could He
Conceive a thing so sad and soft, a gentle thing like me?

I passed a little further on and heard a peacock
    say:

*Who made the grass and made the worms and made my
    feathers gay,*

He is a monstrous peacock, and He waveth all the night
His languid tail above us, lit with myriad spots of light.

The Indian to his Love

Composed 1886
Published in *The Wanderings of Oisin and Other Poems* (1889)
Collected under *Crossways* in his later collections

The island dreams under the dawn
And great boughs drop tranquillity;
The peahens dance on a smooth lawn,
A parrot sways upon a tree,
Raging at his own image in the enamelled sea.

Here we will moor our lonely ship
And wander ever with woven hands,
Murmuring softly lip to lip,
Along the grass, along the sands,
Murmuring how far away are the unquiet lands:

How we alone of mortals are
Hid under quiet boughs apart,
While our love grows an Indian star,
A meteor of the burning heart,
One with the tide that gleams, the wings that
     gleam and dart,

The heavy boughs, the burnished dove
That moans and sighs a hundred days:
How when we die our shades will rove,
When eve has hushed the feathered ways,
With vapoury footsole by the water's drowsy blaze.

The Falling of the Leaves

Published in *The Wanderings of Oisin and Other Poems* (1889)
Collected under *Crossways* in his later collections

Autumn is over the long leaves that love us,
And over the mice in the barley sheaves;
Yellow the leaves of the rowan above us,
And yellow the wet wild-strawberry leaves.

The hour of the waning of love has beset us,
And weary and worn are our sad souls now;
Let us part, ere the season of passion forget us,
With a kiss and a tear on thy drooping brow.

Ephemera

Published in *The Wanderings of Oisin and Other Poems* (1889)
Collected under *Crossways* in his later collections

'Your eyes that once were never weary of mine
Are bowed in sorrow under pendulous lids,
Because our love is waning.'
     And then she:
'Although our love is waning, let us stand
By the lone border of the lake once more,
Together in that hour of gentleness
When the poor tired child, Passion, falls asleep.
How far away the stars seem, and how far
Is our first kiss, and ah, how old my heart!'
Pensive they paced along the faded leaves,
While slowly he whose hand held hers replied:
'Passion has often worn our wandering hearts.'

The woods were round them, and the yellow
  leaves
Fell like faint meteors in the gloom, and once
A rabbit old and lame limped down the path;
Autumn was over him: and now they stood
On the lone border of the lake once more:

Turning, he saw that she had thrust dead leaves
Gathered in silence, dewy as her eyes,
In bosom and hair.

                   'Ah, do not mourn,' he said,
'That we are tired, for other loves await us;
Hate on and love through unrepining hours.
Before us lies eternity; our souls
Are love, and a continual farewell.'

The Madness of King Goll

Published in *The Wanderings of Oisin and Other Poems* (1889)
Collected under *Crossways* in his later collections

I sat on cushioned otter-skin:
My word was law from Ith to Emain,
And shook at Inver Amergin
The hearts of the world-troubling seamen,
And drove tumult and war away
From girl and boy and man and beast;
The fields grew fatter day by day,
The wild fowl of the air increased;
And every ancient Ollave said,
While he bent down his fading head.
'He drives away the Northern cold.'
They will not hush, the leaves a-flutter round me, the beech
leaves old.

I sat and mused and drank sweet wine;
A herdsman came from inland valleys,
Crying, the pirates drove his swine
To fill their dark-beaked hollow galleys.
I called my battle-breaking men
And my loud brazen battle-cars

From rolling vale and rivery glen;
And under the blinking of the stars
Fell on the pirates by the deep,
And hurled them in the gulph of sleep:
These hands won many a torque of gold.
*They will not hush, the leaves a-flutter round me, the beech
    leaves old.*

But slowly, as I shouting slew
And trampled in the bubbling mire,
In my most secret spirit grew
A whirling and a wandering fire:
I stood: keen stars above me shone,
Around me shone keen eyes of men:
I laughed aloud and hurried on
By rocky shore and rushy fen;
I laughed because birds fluttered by,
And starlight gleamed, and clouds flew high,
And rushes waved and waters rolled.
*They will not hush, the leaves a-flutter round me, the beech
    leaves old.*

And now I wander in the woods
When summer gluts the golden bees,
Or in autumnal solitudes
Arise the leopard-coloured trees;
Or when along the wintry strands
The cormorants shiver on their rocks;
I wander on, and wave my hands,
And sing, and shake my heavy locks.
The grey wolf knows me; by one ear
I lead along the woodland deer;

The hares run by me growing bold.
*They will not hush, the leaves a-flutter round me, the beech
    leaves old.*

I came upon a little town
That slumbered in the harvest moon,
And passed a-tiptoe up and down,
Murmuring, to a fitful tune,
How I have followed, night and day,
A tramping of tremendous feet,
And saw where this old tympan lay
Deserted on a doorway seat,
And bore it to the woods with me;
Of some inhuman misery
Our married voices wildly trolled.
*They will not hush, the leaves a-flutter round me, the beech
    leaves old.*

I sang how, when day's toil is done,
Orchil shakes out her long dark hair
That hides away the dying sun
And sheds faint odours through the air:
When my hand passed from wire to wire
It quenched, with sound like falling dew
The whirling and the wandering fire;
But lift a mournful ulalu,
For the kind wires are torn and still,
And I must wander wood and hill
Through summer's heat and winter's cold.
*They will not hush, the leaves a-flutter round me, the beech
    leaves old.*

The Stolen Child

Composed 1886
Published in *The Wanderings of Oisin and Other Poems* (1889)
Collected under *Crossways* in his later collections

Where dips the rocky highland
Of Sleuth Wood in the lake,
There lies a leafy island
Where flapping herons wake
The drowsy water-rats;
There we've hid our faery vats.
Full of berries,
And of reddest stolen cherries.
Come away, O human child!
To the waters and the wild
With a faery, hand in hand,
For the world's more full of weeping than you can understand.

Where the wave of moonlight glosses
The dim grey sands with light,
Far off by furthest Rosses
We foot it all the night,
Weaving olden dances,
Mingling hands and mingling glances

Till the moon has taken flight;
To and fro we leap
And chase the frothy bubbles,
While the world is full of troubles
And is anxious in its sleep.
Come away, O human child!
To the waters and the wild
With a faery, hand in hand,
For the world's more full of weeping than you can understand.

Where the wandering water gushes
From the hills above Glen-Car,
In pools among the rushes
That scarce could bathe a star,
We seek for slumbering trout,
And whispering in their ears
Give them unquiet dreams;
Leaning softly out
From ferns that drop their tears
Over the young streams.
Come away, O human child!
To the waters and the wild
With a faery, hand in hand,
For the world's more full of weeping than you can understand.

Away with us he's going,
The solemn-eyed:
He'll hear no more the lowing
Of the calves on the warm hillside;
Or the kettle on the hob
Sing peace into his breast,

Or see the brown mice bob
Round and round the oatmeal-chest.
For he comes, the human child,
To the waters and the wild
With a faery, hand in hand,
From a world more full of weeping than he can understand.

To an Isle in the Water

Published in *The Wanderings of Oisin and Other Poems* (1889)
Collected under *Crossways* in his later collections

Shy one, shy one,
Shy one of my heart,
She moves in the firelight
Pensively apart.

She carries in the dishes,
And lays them in a row.
To an isle in the water
With her would I go.

She carries in the candles
And lights the curtained room,
Shy in the doorway
And shy in the gloom;

And shy as a rabbit,
Helpful and shy.
To an isle in the water
With her would I fly.

Down by the Salley Gardens

Published in *The Wanderings of Oisin and Other Poems* (1889)
Collected under *Crossways* in his later collections

Down by the salley* gardens my love and I did
    meet;
She passed the salley gardens with little snow-
    white feet.
She bid me take love easy, as the leaves grow on
    the tree;
But I, being young and foolish, with her would
    not agree.

In a field by the river my love and I did stand,
And on my leaning shoulder she laid her snow-
    white hand.
She bid me take life easy, as the grass grows on
    the weirs;
But I was young and foolish, and now am full of
    tears.

---

* Willow

The Ballad of Moll Magee

Published in *The Wanderings of Oisin and Other Poems* (1889)
Collected under *Crossways* in his later collections

Come round me, little childer;
There, don't fling stones at me
Because I mutter as I go;
But pity Moll Magee.

My man was a poor fisher
With shore lines in the say;
My work was saltin' herrings
The whole of the long day.

And sometimes from the saltin' shed
I scarce could drag my feet,
Under the blessed moonlight,
Along the pebbly street.

I'd always been but weakly,
And my baby was just born;
A neighbour minded her by day,
I minded her till morn.

I lay upon my baby;
Ye little childer dear,
I looked on my cold baby
When the morn grew frosty and clear.

A weary woman sleeps so hard!
My man grew red and pale,
And gave me money, and bade me go
To my own place, Kinsale.

He drove me out and shut the door.
And gave his curse to me;
I went away in silence,
No neighbour could I see.

The windows and the doors were shut,
One star shone faint and green,
The little straws were turnin' round
Across the bare boreen.

I went away in silence:
Beyond old Martin's byre
I saw a kindly neighbour
Blowin' her mornin' fire.

She drew from me my story—
My money's all used up,
And still, with pityin', scornin' eye,
She gives me bite and sup.

She says my man will surely come
And fetch me home agin;

But always, as I'm movin' round,
Without doors or within,

Pilin' the wood or pilin' the turf,
Or goin' to the well,
I'm thinkin' of my baby
And keenin' to mysel'.

And sometimes I am sure she knows
When, openin' wide His door,
God lights the stars, His candles,
And looks upon the poor.

So now, ye little childer,
Ye won't fling stones at me;
But gather with your shinin' looks
And pity Moll Magee.

To the Rose upon the Rood of Time

Published in *The Countess Kathleen and Various Legends and Lyrics* (1892)
Collected under *The Rose* in his later collections

Red Rose, proud Rose, sad Rose of all my days!
Come near me, while I sing the ancient ways—
Cuchulain* battling with the bitter tide;
The Druid, grey, wood-nurtured, quiet-eyed,
Who cast round Fergus dreams, and ruin untold;
And thine own sadness, whereof stars, grown old
In dancing silver-sandalled on the sea,
Sing in their high and lonely melody.
Come near, that no more blinded by man's fate,
I find under the boughs of love and hate,
In all poor foolish things that live a day,
Eternal beauty wandering on her way.

Come near, come near, come near—Ah, leave
        me still
A little space for the rose-breath to fill!

---

* The great hero of the Red Branch cycle.

Lest I no more hear common things that crave;
The weak worm hiding down in its small cave—
The field-mouse running by me in the grass,
And heavy mortal hopes that toil and pass;
But seek alone to hear the strange things said
By God to the bright hearts of those long dead,
And learn to chaunt a tongue men do not know.
Come near—I would, before my time to go,
Sing of old Eire and the ancient ways,
Red Rose, proud Rose, sad Rose of all my days.

Fergus and the Druid

Published in *The Countess Kathleen and Various
Legends and Lyrics* (1892)
Collected under *The Rose* in his later collections

FERGUS

This whole day have I followed in the rocks,
And you have changed and flowed from shape
    to shape,
First as a raven on whose ancient wings
Scarcely a feather lingered, then you seemed
A weasel moving on from stone to stone,
And now at last you wear a human shape,
A thin grey man half lost in gathering night.

DRUID

What would you, king of the proud Red Branch
    kings?

FERGUS

This would I say, most wise of living souls:
Young subtle Conchubar sat close by me
When I gave judgment, and his words were wise,
And what to me was burden without end,

To him seemed easy, so I laid the crown
Upon his head to cast away my care.

DRUID

What would you, king of the proud Red Branch
    kings?

FERGUS

A king and proud! and that is my despair.
I feast amid my people on the hill,
And pace the woods, and drive my chariot wheels
In the white border of the murmuring sea;
And still I feel the crown upon my head.

DRUID

What would you?

FERGUS

            Be no more a king
But learn the dreaming wisdom that is yours.

DRUID

Look on my thin grey hair and hollow cheeks
And on these hands that may not lift the sword,
This body trembling like a wind-blown reed.
No woman's loved me, no man sought my help.

FERGUS

A king is but a foolish labourer
Who wastes his blood to be another's dream.

DRUID

Take, if you must, this little bag of dreams;
Unloose the cord, and they will wrap you round.

FERGUS

I see my life go drifting like a river
From change to change; I have been many things—
A green drop in the surge, a gleam of light
Upon a sword, a fir-tree on a hill,
An old slave grinding at a heavy quern,
A king sitting upon a chair of gold—
And all these things were wonderful and great;
But now I have grown nothing, knowing all.
Ah! Druid, Druid, how great webs of sorrow
Lay hidden in the small slate-coloured thing!

Cuchulain's Fight with the Sea

Published in *The Countess Kathleen and Various Legends and Lyrics* (1892) with the title 'The Death of Cuchullin'
Revised and collected under *The Rose* in his later collections with the present title

A man came slowly from the setting sun,
To Emer, raddling raiment in her dun,
And said, 'I am that swineherd whom you bid
Go watch the road between the wood and tide,
But now I have no need to watch it more.'

Then Emer cast the web upon the floor,
And raising arms all raddled with the dye,
Parted her lips with a loud sudden cry.

That swineherd stared upon her face and said,
'No man alive, no man among the dead,
Has won the gold his cars of battle bring.'

'But if your master comes home triumphing
Why must you blench and shake from foot to crown?'

Thereon he shook the more and cast him down
Upon the web-heaped floor, and cried his word:

'With him is one sweet-throated like a bird.'
'You dare me to my face,' and thereupon
She smote with raddled fist, and where her son
Herded the cattle came with stumbling feet,
And cried with angry voice, 'It is not meet
To idle life away, a common herd.'

'I have long waited, mother, for that word:
But wherefore now?'

          'There is a man to die;
You have the heaviest arm under the sky.'

'Whether under its daylight or its stars
My father stands amid his battle-cars.'

'But you have grown to be the taller man.'

'Yet somewhere under starlight or the sun
My father stands.'

           'Aged, worn out with wars
On foot, on horseback or in battle-cars.'

'I only ask what way my journey lies,
For He who made you bitter made you wise.'

'The Red Branch camp in a great company
Between wood's rim and the horses of the sea.
Go there, and light a camp-fire at wood's rim;
But tell your name and lineage to him
Whose blade compels, and wait till they have found

Some feasting man that the same oath has bound.'
Among those feasting men Cuchulain dwelt,
And his young sweetheart close beside him knelt,
Stared on the mournful wonder of his eyes,
Even as Spring upon the ancient skies,
And pondered on the glory of his days;
And all around the harp-string told his praise,
And Conchubar, the Red Branch king of kings,
With his own fingers touched the brazen strings.

At last Cuchulain spake, 'Some man has made
His evening fire amid the leafy shade.
I have often heard him singing to and fro,
I have often heard the sweet sound of his bow.
Seek out what man he is.'

One went and came.
'He bade me let all know he gives his name
At the sword-point, and waits till we have found
Some feasting man that the same oath has bound.'

Cuchulain cried, 'I am the only man
Of all this host so bound from childhood on.'

After short fighting in the leafy shade,
He spake to the young man, 'Is there no maid
Who loves you, no white arms to wrap you round,
Or do you long for the dim sleepy ground,
That you have come and dared me to my face?'
'The dooms of men are in God's hidden place,'

'Your head a while seemed like a woman's head

That I loved once.'
                    Again the fighting sped,
But now the war-rage in Cuchulain woke,
And through that new blade's guard the old blade
    broke,
And pierced him.

                'Speak before your breath is done.'

'Cuchulain I, mighty Cuchulain's son.'

'I put you from your pain. I can no more.'

While day its burden on to evening bore,
With head bowed on his knees Cuchulain stayed;
Then Conchubar sent that sweet-throated maid,
And she, to win him, his grey hair caressed;
In vain her arms, in vain her soft white breast.
Then Conchubar, the subtlest of all men,
Ranking his Druids round him ten by ten,
Spake thus: 'Cuchulain will dwell there and brood
For three days more in dreadful quietude,
And then arise, and raving slay us all.
Chaunt in his ear delusions magical,
That he may fight the horses of the sea.'
The Druids took them to their mystery,
And chaunted for three days.

                Cuchulain stirred,
Stared on the horses of the sea, and heard
The cars of battle and his own name cried;
And fought with the invulnerable tide.

A Faery Song

Published in *The Countess Kathleen and*
Various Legends and Lyrics (1892)
Collected under *The Rose* in his later collections

Sung by the people of Faery over Diarmuid and Grania, in
their bridal sleep under a Cromlech.

We who are old, old and gay,
O so old!
Thousands of years, thousands of years,
If all were told:

Give to these children, new from the world,
Silence and love;
And the long dew-dropping hours of the night,
And the stars above:

Give to these children, new from the world,
Rest far from men.
Is anything better, anything better?
Tell us it then:

Us who are old, old and gay,
O so old!
Thousands of years, thousands of years,
If all were told.

The Lake Isle of Innisfree

Composed 1888
Published in *The Countess Kathleen and
Various Legends and Lyrics* (1892)
Collected under *The Rose* in his later collections

I will arise and go now, and go to Innisfree,
And a small cabin build there, of clay and wattles made:
Nine bean-rows will I have there, a hive for the
　　honey-bee,
And live alone in the bee-loud glade.

And I shall have some peace there, for peace
　　comes dropping slow,
Dropping from the veils of the morning to where
　　the cricket sings;
There midnight's all a glimmer, and noon a purple glow,
And evening full of the linnet's wings.

I will arise and go now, for always night and day
I hear lake water lapping with low sounds by the shore;
While I stand on the roadway, or on the pavements
　　grey,
I hear it in the deep heart's core.

A Cradle Song

Published in *The Countess Kathleen and
Various Legends and Lyrics* (1892)
Revised and collected under *The Rose* in his later collections

The angels are stooping
Above your bed;
They weary of trooping
With the whimpering dead.

God's laughing in heaven
To see you so good;
The Sailing Seven
Are gay with His mood.

I sigh that kiss you,
For I must own;
That I shall miss you
When you have grown.

The Pity of Love

Published in *The Countess Kathleen and
Various Legends and Lyrics* (1892)
Revised and collected under *The Rose* in his later collections

A pity beyond all telling
Is hid in the heart of love:
The folk who are buying and selling,
The clouds on their journey above,
The cold, wet winds ever blowing,
And the shadowy hazel grove
Where mouse-grey waters are flowing
Threaten the head that I love.

The Sorrow of Love

Published in *The Countess Kathleen and
Various Legends and Lyrics* (1892)
Revised and collected under *The Rose* in his later collections

The brawling of a sparrow in the eaves,
The brilliant moon and all the milky sky,
And all that famous harmony of leaves,
Had blotted out man's image and his cry.

A girl arose that had red mournful lips
And seemed the greatness of the world in tears,
Doomed like Odysseus and the labouring ships
And proud as Priam murdered with his peers;

Arose, and on the instant clamorous eaves,
A climbing moon upon an empty sky,
And all that lamentation of the leaves,
Could but compose man's image and his cry.

When You Are Old

Composed 1891
Published in *The Countess Kathleen and
Various Legends and Lyrics* (1892)
Revised and collected under *The Rose* in his later collections

When you are old and grey and full of sleep,
And nodding by the fire, take down this book,
And slowly read, and dream of the soft look
Your eyes had once, and of their shadows deep.

How many loved your moments of glad grace,
And loved your beauty with love false or true;
But one man loved the pilgrim soul in you,
And loved the sorrows of your changing face.

And bending down beside the glowing bars
Murmur, a little sadly, how Love fled
And paced upon the mountains overhead
And hid his face amid a crowd of stars.

The White Birds

Composed 1892
Published in *The Countess Kathleen and
Various Legends and Lyrics* (1892)
Revised and collected under *The Rose* in his later collections

I would that we were, my beloved, white birds on
    the foam of the sea!
We tire of the flame of the meteor, before it can
    fade and flee;
And the flame of the blue star of twilight, hung
    low on the rim of the sky,
Has awakened in our hearts, my beloved, a
    sadness that may not die.

A weariness comes from those dreamers, dew-
    dabbled, the lily and rose;
Ah, dream not of them, my beloved, the flame of
    the meteor that goes,
Or the flame of the blue star that lingers hung low
    in the fall of the dew:
For I would we were changed to white birds on
    the wandering foam: I and you!

I am haunted by numberless islands, and many a
    Danaan shore,
Where Time would surely forget us, and Sorrow
    come near us no more;
Soon far from the rose and the lily, and fret of the
    flames would we be,
Were we only white birds, my beloved, buoyed out
    on the foam of the sea!

Who goes with Fergus?

Published in *The Countess Kathleen and
Various Legends and Lyrics* (1892)
Collected under *The Rose* in his later collections

Who will go drive with Fergus now,
And pierce the deep wood's woven shade,
And dance upon the level shore?
Young man, lift up your russet brow,
And lift your tender eyelids, maid,
And brood on hopes and fear no more.

And no more turn aside and brood
Upon love's bitter mystery;
For Fergus rules the brazen cars,
And rules the shadows of the wood,
And the white breast of the dim sea
And all dishevelled wandering stars.

The Man who dreamed of Faeryland

Composed 1892
Published in *The Countess Kathleen and
Various Legends and Lyrics* (1892)
Collected under *The Rose* in his later collections

He stood among a crowd at Dromahair;
His heart hung all upon a silken dress,
And he had known at last some tenderness,
Before earth took him to her stony care;
But when a man poured fish into a pile,
It seemed they raised their little silver heads,
And sang what gold morning or evening sheds
Upon a woven world-forgotten isle
Where people love beside the ravelled seas;
That Time can never mar a lover's vows
Under that woven changeless roof of boughs:
The singing shook him out of his new ease.

He wandered by the sands of Lissadell;
His mind ran all on money cares and fears,
And he had known at last some prudent years
Before they heaped his grave under the hill;
But while he passed before a plashy place,
A lug-worm with its grey and muddy mouth

Sang that somewhere to north or west or south
There dwelt a gay, exulting, gentle race
Under the golden or the silver skies;
That if a dancer stayed his hungry foot
It seemed the sun and moon were in the fruit:
And at that singing he was no more wise.

He mused beside the well of Scanavin,
He mused upon his mockers: without fail
His sudden vengeance were a country tale,
When earthy night had drunk his body in;
But one small knot-grass growing by the pool
Sang where—unnecessary cruel voice—
Old silence bids its chosen race rejoice,
Whatever ravelled waters rise and fall
Or stormy silver fret the gold of day,
And midnight there enfold them like a fleece
And lover there by lover be at peace.
The tale drove his fine angry mood away.

He slept under the hill of Lugnagall;
And might have known at last unhaunted sleep
Under that cold and vapour-turbaned steep,
Now that the earth had taken man and all:
Did not the worms that spired about his bones
proclaim with that unwearied, reedy cry
That God has laid His fingers on the sky,
That from those fingers glittering summer runs
Upon the dancer by the dreamless wave.
Why should those lovers that no lovers miss
Dream, until God burn Nature with a kiss?
The man has found no comfort in the grave.

The Lamentation of the Old Pensioner

Published in *The Countess Kathleen and
Various Legends and Lyrics* (1892)
Revised and collected under *The Rose* in his later collections

Although I shelter from the rain
Under a broken tree
My chair was nearest to the fire
In every company
That talked of love or politics,
Ere Time transfigured me.

Though lads are making pikes again
For some conspiracy,
And crazy rascals rage their fill
At human tyranny,
My contemplations are of Time
That has transfigured me.

There's not a woman turns her face
Upon a broken tree,

And yet the beauties that I loved
Are in my memory;
I spit into the face of Time
That has transfigured me.

The Ballad of Father Gilligan

Published in *The Countess Kathleen and
Various Legends and Lyrics* (1892)
Collected under *The Rose* in his later collections

The old priest Peter Gilligan
Was weary night and day;
For half his flock were in their beds,
Or under green sods lay.

Once, while he nodded in a chair;
At the moth-hour of the eve,
Another poor man sent for him,
And he began to grieve.

'I have no rest, nor joy, nor peace,
For people die and die';
And after cried he, 'God forgive!
My body spake, not I!'

He knelt, and leaning on the chair
He prayed and fell asleep;
And the moth-hour went from the fields,
And stars began to peep.

They slowly into millions grew,
And leaves shook in the wind;
And God covered the world with shade,
And whispered to mankind.

Upon the time of sparrow chirp
When the moths came once more,
The old priest Peter Gilligan
Stood upright on the floor.

'Mavrone, mavrone! The man has died
While I slept in the chair.'
He roused his horse out of its sleep
And rode with little care.

He rode now as he never rode,
By rocky lane and fen;
The sick man's wife opened the door,
'Father! you come again!'

'And is the poor man dead?' he cried
'He died an hour ago.'
The old priest Peter Gilligan
In grief swayed to and fro.

'When you were gone, he turned and died,
As merry as a bird.'
The old priest Peter Gilligan
He knelt him at that word.

'He Who hath made the night of stars
For souls who tire and bleed,

Sent one of this great angels down,
To help me in my need.

'He Who is wrapped in purple robes,
With planets in His care
Had pity on the least of things
Asleep upon a chair.'

To Ireland in the Coming Times

Published in *The Countess Kathleen and Various
Legends and Lyrics* (1892) with the title 'Apologia addressed to
Ireland in the coming days'
Revised and collected under *The Rose* in his later collections
with the present title

Know, that I would accounted be
True brother of a company
That sang, to sweeten Ireland's wrong,
Ballad and story, rann and song;
Nor be I any less of them,
Because the red-rose-bordered hem
Of her, whose history began
Before God made the angelic clan,
Trails all about the written page.
When Time began to rant and rage
The measure of her flying feet
Made Ireland's heart begin to beat;
And Time bade all his candles flare
To light a measure here and there;
And may the thoughts of Ireland brood
Upon a measured quietude.

Nor may I less be counted one

With Davis, Mangan, Ferguson,
Because, to him who ponders well,
My rhymes more than their rhyming tell
Of things discovered in the deep,
Where only body's laid asleep.
For the elemental creatures go
About my table to and fro,
That hurry from unmeasured mind
To rant and rage in flood and wind;
Yet he who treads in measured ways
May surely barter gaze for gaze.
Man ever journeys on with them
After the red-rose-bordered hem.
Ah, faeries, dancing under the moon,
A Druid land, a Druid tune!

While still I may, I write for you
The love I lived, the dream I knew.
From our birthday, until we die,
Is but the winking of an eye;
And we, our singing and our love,
What measurer Time has lit above,
And all benighted things that go
About my table to and fro,
Are passing on to where may be,
In truth's consuming ecstasy,
No place for love and dream at all;
For God goes by with white footfall.
I cast my heart into my rhymes,
That you, in the dim coming times,
May know how my heart went with them
After the red-rose-bordered hem.

To Some I Have Talked with by the Fire

Published in *Poems* (1895)
Collected under *The Rose* in his later collections

While I wrought out these fitful Danaan rhymes,
My heart would brim with dreams about the times
When we bent down above the fading coals
And talked of the dark folk who live in souls
Of passionate men, like bats in the dead trees;
And of the wayward twilight companies
Who sigh with mingled sorrow and content,
Because their blossoming dreams have never bent
Under the fruit of evil and of good:
And of the embattled flaming multitude
Who rise, wing above wing, flame above flame,
And, like a storm, cry the Ineffable Name,
And with the clashing of their sword-blades make
A rapturous music, till the morning break
And the white hush end all but the loud beat
Of their long wings, the flash of their white feet.

The Hosting of the Sidhe*

From *The Wind Among the Reeds* (1899)

The host is riding from Knocknarea
And over the grave of Clooth-na-bare;
Caolte tossing his burning hair
And Niamh calling *Away, come away:*
Empty your heart of its mortal dream.
The winds awaken, the leaves whirl round,
Our cheeks are pale, our hair is unbound,
Our breasts are heaving, our eyes are a-gleam,
Our arms are waving, our lips are apart;
And if any gaze on our rushing band,
We come between him and the deed of his hand,
We come between him and the hope of his heart.
The host is rushing 'twixt night and day,
And where is there hope or deed as fair?
Caolte tossing his burning hair,
And Niamh calling *Away, come away.*

---

* The faery people. The word is also Gaelic for wind.

Aedh tells of the Rose in his Heart

From The Wind Among the Reeds (1899)
Later entitled 'The Lover Tells of the Rose in his Heart'

All things uncomely and broken, all things worn
    out and old,
The cry of a child by the roadway, the creak of a
    lumbering cart,
The heavy steps of the ploughman, splashing the
    wintry mould,
Are wronging your image that blossoms a rose in
    the deeps of my heart.

The wrong of unshapely things is a wrong too
    great to be told;
I hunger to build them anew and sit on a green
    knoll apart,
With the earth and the sky and the water, remade,
    like a casket of gold
For my dreams of your image that blossoms a
    rose in the deeps of my heart.

The Host of the Air

From *The Wind Among the Reeds* (1899)

O'Driscoll drove with a song,
The wild duck and the drake,
From the tall and the tufted reeds
Of the drear Hart Lake.

And he saw how the reeds grew dark
At the coming of night tide,
And dreamed of the long dim hair
Of Bridget his bride.

He heard while he sang and dreamed
A piper piping away,
And never was piping so sad,
And never was piping so gay.

And he saw young men and young girls
Who danced on a level place
And Bridget his bride among them,
With a sad and a gay face.

The dancers crowded about him,
And many a sweet thing said,
And a young man brought him red wine
And a young girl white bread.

But Bridget drew him by the sleeve,
Away from the merry bands,
To old men playing at cards
With a twinkling of ancient hands.

The bread and the wine had a doom,
For these were the host of the air;
He sat and played in a dream
Of her long dim hair.

He played with the merry old men
And thought not of evil chance,
Until one bore Bridget his bride
Away from the merry dance.

He bore her away in his arms,
The handsomest young man there,
And his neck and his breast and his arms
Were drowned in her long dim hair.

O'Driscoll scattered the cards
And out of his dream awoke:
Old men and young men and young girls
Were gone like a drifting smoke;

But he heard high up in the air
A piper piping away,
And never was piping so sad,
And never was piping so gay.

Into the Twilight

From *The Wind Among the Reeds* (1899)

Out-worn heart, in a time out-worn,
Come clear of the nets of wrong and right;
Laugh, heart, again in the grey twilight,
Sigh, heart, again in the dew of the morn.

Your mother Eire is always young,
Dew ever shining and twilight grey;
Though hope fall from you and love decay,
Burning in fires of a slanderous tongue.

Come, heart, where hill is heaped upon hill:
For there the mystical brotherhood
Of sun and moon and hollow and wood
And river and stream work out their will;

And God stands winding His lonely horn,
And time and the world are ever in flight;
And love is less kind than the grey twilight,
And hope is less dear than the dew of the morn.

The Song of Wandering Aengus

From *The Wind Among the Reeds* (1899)

I went out to the hazel wood,
Because a fire was in my head,
And cut and peeled a hazel wand,
And hooked a berry to a thread;
And when white moths were on the wing,
And moth-like stars were flickering out,
I dropped the berry in a stream
And caught a little silver trout.

When I had laid it on the floor
I went to blow the fire a-flame,
But something rustled on the floor,
And someone called me by my name:
It had become a glimmering girl
With apple blossom in her hair
Who called me by my name and ran
And faded through the brightening air.

Though I am old with wandering
Through hollow lands and hilly lands,
I will find out where she has gone,

And kiss her lips and take her hands;
And walk among long dappled grass,
And pluck till time and times are done,
The silver apples of the moon,
The golden apples of the sun.

The Song of the Old Mother

From *The Wind Among the Reeds* (1899)

I rise in the dawn, and I kneel and blow
Till the seed of the fire flicker and glow;
And then I must scrub and bake and sweep
Till stars are beginning to blink and peep;
And the young lie long and dream in their bed
Of the matching of ribbons for bosom and head,
And their day goes over in idleness,
And they sigh if the wind but lift a tress:
While I must work because I am old,
And the seed of the fire gets feeble and cold.

The Heart of the Woman

From *The Wind Among the Reeds* (1899)

O what to me the little room
That was brimmed up with prayer and rest;
He bade me out into the gloom,
And my breast lies upon his breast.

O what to me my mother's care,
The house where I was safe and warm;
The shadowy blossom of my hair
Will hide us from the bitter storm.

O hiding hair and dewy eyes,
I am no more with life and death,
My heart upon his warm heart lies,
My breath is mixed into his breath.

The Fiddler of Dooney

From *The Wind Among the Reeds* (1899)

When I play on my fiddle in Dooney,
Folk dance like a wave of the sea;
My cousin is priest in Kilvarnet,
My brother in Moharabuiee.

I passed my brother and cousin:
They read in their books of prayer;
I read in my book of songs
I bought at the Sligo fair.

When we come at the end of time,
To Peter sitting in state,
He will smile on the three old spirits,
But call me first through the gate;

For the good are always the merry,
Save by an evil chance,
And the merry love the fiddle
And the merry love to dance:

And when the folk there spy me,
They will all come up to me,
With 'Here is the fiddler of Dooney!'
And dance like a wave of the sea.

Aedh laments the
Loss of Love

From *The Wind Among the Reeds* (1899)
Later entitled 'The Lover mourns for the Loss of Love'

Pale brows, still hands and dim hair,
I had a beautiful friend
And dreamed that the old despair
Would end in love in the end:
She looked in my heart one day
And saw your image was there;
She has gone weeping away.

Michael Robartes remembers forgotten Beauty

From *The Wind Among the Reeds* (1899)
Later entitled 'He remembers forgotten Beauty'

When my arms wrap you round I press
My heart upon the loveliness
That has long faded from the world;
The jewelled crowns that kings have hurled
In shadowy pools, when armies fled;
The love-tales wove with silken thread
By dreaming ladies upon cloth
That has made fat the murderous moth;
The roses that of old time were
Woven by ladies in their hair,
The dew-cold lilies ladies bore
Through many a sacred corridor
Where such grey clouds of incense rose
That only the Gods' eyes did not close:
For that pale breast and lingering hand
Come from a more dream-heavy land,
A more dream-heavy hour than this;
And when you sigh from kiss to kiss

I hear white Beauty sighing, too,
For hours when all must fade like dew
But flame on flame, deep under deep,
Throne over throne, where in half sleep
Their swords upon their iron knees
Brood her high lonely mysteries.

A Poet to his Beloved

From *The Wind Among the Reeds* (1899)

I bring you with reverent hands
The books of my numberless dreams;
White woman that passion has worn
As the tide wears the dove-grey sands,
And with heart more old than the horn
That is brimmed from the pale fire of time:
White woman with numberless dreams
I bring you my passionate rhyme.

Aedh gives his Beloved certain Rhymes

From *The Wind Among the Reeds* (1899)
Later entitled 'He gives his Beloved certain Rhymes'

Fasten your hair with a golden pin,
And bind up every wandering tress;
I bade my heart build these poor rhymes:
It worked at them, day out, day in,
Building a sorrowful loveliness
Out of the battles of old times.

You need but lift a pearl-pale hand,
And bind up your long hair and sigh;
And all men's hearts must burn and beat;
And candle-like foam on the dim sand,
And stars climbing the dew-dropping sky,
Live but to light your passing feet.

The Cap and Bells

From *The Wind Among the Reeds* (1899)

The jester walked in the garden:
The garden had fallen still;
He bade his soul rise upward
And stand on her window-sill.

It rose in a straight blue garment,
When owls began to call:
It had grown wise-tongued by thinking
Of a quiet and light footfall;

But the young queen would not listen;
She rose in her pale night gown;
She drew in the heavy casement
And pushed the latches down.

He bade his heart go to her,
When the owls called out no more;
In a red and quivering garment
It sang to her through the door.

It had grown sweet-tongued by dreaming,
Of a flutter of flower-like hair;
But she took up her fan from the table
And waved it off on the air.

'I have cap and bells,' he pondered,
'I will send them to her and die;'
And when the morning whitened
He left them where she went by.

She laid them upon her bosom,
Under a cloud of her hair,
And her red lips sang them a love song:
Till stars grew out of the air.

She opened her door and her window,
And the heart and the soul came through,
To her right hand came the red one,
To her left hand came the blue.

They set up a noise like crickets,
A chattering wise and sweet,
And her hair was a folded flower
And the quiet of love in her feet.

Aedh tells of a
valley full of Lovers

From *The Wind Among the Reeds* (1899)
Later entitled 'He tells of a valley full of Lovers'

I dreamed that I stood in a valley, and amid sighs,
For happy lovers passed two by two where I stood;
And I dreamed my lost love came stealthily out of
    the wood
With her cloud-pale eyelids falling on dream-
    dimmed eyes:
I cried in my dream, '*O women, bid the young men lay*
Their heads on your knees, and drown their eyes with your
    hair,
Or remembering hers they will find no other face fair
Till all the valleys of the world have been withered away.'

Aedh tells of
the Perfect Beauty

From *The Wind Among the Reeds* (1899)
Later entitled 'He tells of the Perfect Beauty'

O cloud-pale eyelids, dream-dimmed eyes
The poets labouring all their days
To build a perfect beauty in rhyme
Are overthrown by a woman's gaze
And by the unlabouring brood of the skies:
And therefore my heart will bow, when dew
Is dropping sleep, until God burn time,
Before the unlabouring stars and you.

Aedh thinks of Those who have spoken Evil of his Beloved

From *The Wind Among the Reeds* (1899)
Later entitled 'He thinks of Those who have spoken
Evil of his Beloved'

Half close your eyelids, loosen your hair,
And dream about the great and their pride;
They have spoken against you everywhere,
But weigh this song with the great and their pride;
I made it out of a mouthful of air,
Their children's children shall say they have lied.

The Poet pleads with his Friend for Old Friends

From *The Wind Among the Reeds* (1899)
Later entitled 'The Lover pleads with his Friend for Old Friends'

Though you are in your shining days,
Voices among the crowd
And new friends busy with your praise,
Be not unkind or proud,
But think about old friends the most:
Time's bitter flood will rise,
Your beauty perish and be lost
For all eyes but these eyes.

Aedh wishes
his Beloved were Dead

From *The Wind Among the Reeds* (1899)
Later entitled 'He wishes his Beloved were Dead'

Were you but lying cold and dead,
And lights were paling out of the West,
You would come hither, and bend your head,
And I would lay my head on your breast;
And you would murmur tender words,
Forgiving me, because you were dead:
Nor would you rise and hasten away,
Though you have the will of the wild birds,
But know your hair was bound and wound
About the stars and moon and sun:
O would, beloved, that you lay
Under the dock-leaves in the ground,
While lights were paling one by one.

Aedh wishes for the Cloths of Heaven

From *The Wind Among the Reeds* (1899)
Later entitled 'He wishes for the Cloths of Heaven'

Had I the heavens' embroidered cloths,
Enwrought with golden and silver light,
The blue and the dim and the dark cloths
Of night and light and the half-light,
I would spread the cloths under your feet:
But I, being poor, have only my dreams;
I have spread my dreams under your feet;
Tread softly because you tread on my dreams.

In the Seven Woods

From *In the Seven Woods* (1903)

I have heard the pigeons of the Seven Woods
Make their faint thunder, and the garden bees
Hum in the lime-tree flowers; and put away
The unavailing outcries and the old bitterness
That empty the heart. I have forgot awhile
Tara uprooted, and new commonness
Upon the throne and crying about the streets
And hanging its paper flowers from post to post,
Because it is alone of all things happy.
I am contented, for I know that Quiet
Wanders laughing and eating her wild heart
Among pigeons and bees, while that Great
Archer,
Who but awaits His hour to shoot, still hangs
A cloudy quiver over Pairc-na-Lee.

August 1902

Baile and Aillinn

From *In the Seven Woods* (1903)

Argument. Baile and Aillinn were lovers, but Aengus, the
Master of Love, wishing them to be happy in his own land
among the dead, told to each a story of the other's death,
so that their hearts were broken and they died.

I hardly hear the curlew cry,
Nor the grey rush when wind is high,
Before my thoughts begin to run
On the heir of Ulad, Buan's son,
Baile who had the honey mouth,
And that mild woman of the south,
Aillinn, who was King Lugaid's heir.
Their love was never drowned in care
Of this or that thing, nor grew cold
Because their bodies had grown old;
Being forbid to marry on earth
They blossomed to immortal mirth.

About the time when Christ was born,
When the long wars for the White Horn
And the Brown Bull had not yet come,

Young Baile Honey-Mouth, whom some
Called rather Baile Little-Land,
Rode out of Emain with a band
Of harpers and young men, and they
Imagined, as they struck the way
To many pastured Muirthemne,
That all things fell out happily
And there, for all that fools had said,
Baile and Aillinn would be wed.

They found an old man running there,
He had ragged long grass-yellow hair;
He had knees that stuck out of his hose;
He had puddle water in his shoes;
He had half a cloak to keep him dry;
Although he had a squirrel's eye.

O wandering birds and rushy beds
You put such folly in our heads
With all this crying in the wind
No common love is to our mind,
And our poor Kate or Nan is less
Than any whose unhappiness
Awoke the harp strings long ago.
Yet they that know all things but know
That all life had to give us is
A child's laughter, a woman's kiss.
Who was it put so great a scorn
In the grey reeds that night and morn
Are trodden and broken by the herds,
And in the light bodies of birds

That north wind tumbles to and fro
And pinches among hail and snow?

That runner said, 'I am from the south;
I run to Baile Honey-Mouth
To tell him how the girl Aillinn
Rode from the country of her kin
And old and young men rode with her:
For all that country had been astir
If anybody half as fair
Had chosen a husband anywhere
But where it could see her every day.
When they had ridden a little way
An old man caught the horse's head
With "You must home again and wed
With somebody in your own land."
A young man cried and kissed her hand
"O lady, wed with one of us;"
And when no face grew piteous
For any gentle thing she spake
She fell and died of the heart-break.'

Because a lover's heart's worn out
Being tumbled and blown about
By its own blind imagining,
And will believe that anything
That is bad enough to be true, is true,
Baile's heart was broken in two;
And he being laid upon green boughs
Was carried to the goodly house
Where the Hound of Ulad sat before

The brazen pillars of his door;
His face bowed low to weep the end
Of the harper's daughter and her friend;
For although years had passed away
He always wept them on that day,
For on that day they had been betrayed;
And now that Honey-Mouth is laid
Under a cairn of sleepy stone
Before his eyes, he has tears for none,
Although he is carrying stone, but two
For whom the cairn's but heaped anew.

We hold because our memory is
So full of that thing and of this
That out of sight is out of mind.
But the grey rush under the wind
And the grey bird with crooked bill
Have such long memories that they still
Remember Deirdre and her man,
And when we walk with Kate or Nan
About the windy water side
Our heart can hear the voices chide.
How could we be so soon content
Who know the way that Naoise went?
And they have news of Deirdre's eyes
Who being lovely was so wise,
Ah wise, my heart knows well how wise.

Now had that old gaunt crafty one,
Gathering his cloak about him, run
Where Aillinn rode with waiting maids
Who amid leafy lights and shades

Dreamed of the hands that would unlace
Their bodices in some dim place
When they had come to the marriage bed;
And harpers pondering with bowed head
A music that had thought enough
Of the ebb of all things to make love
Grow gentle without sorrowings;
And leather-coated men with slings
Who peered about on every side;
And amid leafy light he cried,
'He is well out of wind and wave,
They have heaped the stones above his grave
In Muirthemne and over it
In changeless Ogham letters writ
Baile that was of Rury's seed.
But the gods long ago decreed
No waiting maid should ever spread
Baile and Aillinn's marriage bed,
For they should clip and clip again
Where wild bees hive on the Great Plain.
Therefore it is but little news
That put this hurry in my shoes.'

And hurrying to the south he came
To that high hill the herdsmen name
The Hill Seat of Leighin, because
Some god or king had made the laws
That held the land together there,
In old times among the clouds of the air.

That old man climbed; the day grew dim;
Two swans came flying up to him

Linked by a gold chain each to each
And with low murmuring laughing speech
Alighted on the windy grass.
They knew him: his changed body was
Tall, proud and ruddy, and light wings
Were hovering over the harp strings
That Etain, Midhir's wife, had wove
In the hid place, being crazed by love.

What shall I call them? fish that swim
Scale rubbing scale where light is dim
By a broad water-lily leaf;
Or mice in the one wheaten sheaf
Forgotten at the threshing place;
Or birds lost in the one clear space
Of morning light in a dim sky;
Or it may be, the eyelids of one eye
Or the door pillars of one house,
Or two sweet blossoming apple boughs
That have one shadow on the ground;
Or the two strings that made one sound
Where that wise harper's finger ran;
For this young girl and this young man
Have happiness without an end
Because they have made so good a friend.

They know all wonders, for they pass
The towery gates of Gorias
And Findrias and Falias
And long-forgotten Murias,
Among the giant kings whose hoard
Cauldron and spear and stone and sword

Was robbed before Earth gave the wheat;
Wandering from broken street to street
They come where some huge watcher is
And tremble with their love and kiss.

They know undying things, for they
Wander where earth withers away,
Though nothing troubles the great streams
But light from the pale stars, and gleams
From the holy orchards, where there is none
But fruit that is of precious stone,
Or apples of the sun and moon.

What were our praise to them: they eat
Quiet's wild heart, like daily meat,
Who when night thickens are afloat
On dappled skins in a glass boat
Far out under a windless sky,
While over them birds of Aengus fly,
And over the tiller and the prow
And waving white wings to and fro
Awaken wanderings of light air
To stir their coverlet and their hair.

And poets found, old writers say,
A yew tree where his body lay,
But a wild apple hid the grass
With its sweet blossom where hers was;
And being in good heart, because
A better time had come again
After the deaths of many men,
And that long fighting at the ford,

They wrote on tablets of thin board,
Made of the apple and the yew,
All the love stories that they knew.

Let rush and bird cry out their fill
Of the harper's daughter if they will,
Beloved, I am not afraid of her
She is not wiser nor lovelier,
And you are more high of heart than she
For all her wanderings over-sea;
But I'd have bird and rush forget
Those other two, for never yet
Has lover lived but longed to wive
Like them that are no more alive.

The Arrow

As collected under *In the Seven Woods*
in *Later Poems* (1922)

I thought of your beauty, and this arrow,
Made out of a wild thought, is in my marrow.
There's no man may look upon her, no man;
As when newly grown to be a woman,
Tall and noble but with face and bosom
Delicate in colour as apple blossom.
This beauty's kinder, yet for a reason
I could weep that the old is out of season.

The Folly of being Comforted

As collected under *In the Seven Woods*
in *Later Poems* (1922)

One that is ever kind said yesterday:
'Your well-beloved's hair has threads of grey
And little shadows come about her eyes;
Time can but make it easier to be wise
Though now it seem possible, and so
Patience is all that you have need of.'

                      No,
I have not a crumb of comfort, not a grain,
Time can but make her beauty over again:
Because of that great nobleness of hers
The fire that stirs about her, when she stirs
Burns but more clearly. O she had not these ways,
When all the wild summer was in her gaze.
O heart! O heart! if she'd but turn her head,
You'd know the folly of being comforted.

Never give all the Heart

As collected under *In the Seven Woods*
in *Later Poems* (1922)

Never give all the heart, for love
Will hardly seem worth thinking of
To passionate women if it seem
Certain, and they never dream
That it fades out from kiss to kiss;
For everything that's lovely is
But a brief dreamy kind delight.
O never give the heart outright,
For they, for all smooth lips can say,
Have given their hearts up to the play.
And who could play it well enough
If deaf and dumb and blind with love?
He that made this knows all the cost,
For he gave all his heart and lost.

Adam's Curse

As collected under *In the Seven Woods*
in *Later Poems* (1922)

We sat together at one summer's end,
That beautiful mild woman, your close friend,
And you and I, and talked of poetry.
I said: 'A line will take us hours maybe;
Yet if it does not seem a moment's thought,
Our stitching and unstitching has been naught.
Better go down upon your marrow bones
And scrub a kitchen pavement, or break stones
Like an old pauper, in all kinds of weather;
For to articulate sweet sounds together
Is to work harder than all these, and yet
Be thought an idler by the noisy set
Of bankers, schoolmasters, and clergymen
The martyrs call the world.'

     And thereupon
That beautiful mild woman for whose sake
There's many a one shall find out all heartache
On finding that her voice is sweet and low
Replied: 'To be born woman is to know,

Although they do not talk of it at school—
That we must labour to be beautiful.'
I said: 'It's certain there is no fine thing
Since Adam's fall but needs much labouring.
There have been lovers who thought love should be
So much compounded of high courtesy
That they would sigh and quote with learned looks
Precedents out of beautiful old books;
Yet now it seems an idle trade enough.'

We sat grown quiet at the name of love;
We saw the last embers of daylight die,
And in the trembling blue-green of the sky
A moon, worn as if it had been a shell
Washed by time's waters as they rose and fell
About the stars and broke in days and years.

I had a thought for no one's but your ears;
That you were beautiful, and that I strove
To love you in the old high way of love;
That it had all seemed happy, and yet we'd grown
As weary hearted as that hollow moon.

The Song of Red Hanrahan

From *In the Seven Woods* (1903)

The old brown thorn trees break in two high over
    Cummen Strand
Under a bitter black wind that blows from the left
    hand,
Our courage breaks like an old tree in a black
    wind and dies;
But we have hidden in our hearts the flame out of
    the eyes
Of Cathleen, the daughter of Houlihan.

The wind has bundled up the clouds high over
    Knocknarea
And thrown the thunder on the stones for all that
    Maeve can say.
Angers that are like noisy clouds have set our
    hearts abeat;
But we have all bent low and low and kissed the
    quiet feet
Of Cathleen, the daughter of Houlihan.

The yellow pool has overflowed high up on Clooth-
    na-Bare,
For the wet winds are blowing out of the clinging
    air;
Like heavy flooded waters our bodies and our
    blood;
But purer than a tall candle before the Holy Rood
Is Cathleen, the daughter of Houlihan.

O do not love too Long

As collected under *In the Seven Woods*
in *Later Poems* (1922)

Sweetheart, do not love too long:
I loved long and long,
And grew to be out of fashion
Like an old song.

All through the years of our youth
Neither could have known
Their own thought from the other's,
We were so much at one.

But O, in a minute she changed—
O do not love too long,
Or you will grow out of fashion
Like an old song.

The Happy Townland

As collected under *In the Seven Woods*
in *Later Poems* (1922)

There's many a strong farmer
Whose heart would break in two,
If he could see the townland
That we are riding to;
Boughs have their fruit and blossom
At all times of the year;
Rivers are running over
With red beer and brown beer.
An old man plays the bagpipes
In a golden and silver wood;
Queens, their eyes blue like the ice,
Are dancing in a crowd.

The little fox he murmured,
'O what of the world's bane?'
The sun was laughing sweetly,
The moon plucked at my rein;
But the little red fox murmured,
'O do not pluck at his rein,
He is riding to the townland

That is the world's bane.'
When their hearts are so high
That they would come to blows,
They unhook their heavy swords
From golden and silver boughs;
But all that are killed in battle
Awaken to life again.
It is lucky that their story
Is not known among men,
For O, the strong farmers
That would let the spade lie,
Their hearts would be like a cup
That somebody had drunk dry.

The little fox he murmured,
'O what of the world's bane?'
The sun was laughing sweetly,
The moon plucked at my rein;
But the little red fox murmured,
'O do not pluck at his rein,
He is riding to the townland
That is the world's bane.'

Michael will unhook his trumpet
From a bough overhead,
And blow a little noise
When the supper has been spread.
Gabriel will come from the water
With a fish tail, and talk
Of wonders that have happened
On wet roads where men walk,
And lift up an old horn

Of hammered silver, and drink
Till he has fallen asleep
Upon the starry brink.

The little fox he murmured,
'O what of the world's bane?'
The sun was laughing sweetly,
The moon plucked at my rein;
But the little red fox murmured,
'O do not pluck at his rein,
He is riding to the townland
That is the world's bane.'

No Second Troy

From *The Green Helmet and Other Poems* (1912)

Why should I blame her that she filled my days
With misery, or that she would of late
Have taught to ignorant men most violent ways,
Or hurled the little streets upon the great,
Had they but courage equal to desire?
What could have made her peaceful with a mind
That nobleness made simple as a fire,
With beauty like a tightened bow, a kind
That is not natural in an age like this,
Being high and solitary and most stern?
Why, what could she have done, being what she is?
Was there another Troy for her to burn?

Reconciliation

From *The Green Helmet and Other Poems* (1912)

Some may have blamed you that you took away
The verses that could move them on the day
When, the ears being deafened, the sight of the
    eyes blind
With lightning, you went from me, and I could find
Nothing to make a song about but kings,
Helmets, and swords, and half-forgotten things
That were like memories of you—but now
We'll out, for the world lives as long ago;
And while we're in our laughing, weeping fit,
Hurl helmets, crowns, and swords into the pit.
But, dear, cling close to me; since you were gone,
My barren thoughts have chilled me to the bone.

A Drinking Song

From *The Green Helmet and Other Poems* (1912)

Wine comes in at the mouth
And love comes in at the eye;
That's all we shall know for truth
Before we grow old and die.
I lift the glass to my mouth,
I look at you, and I sigh.

The Coming of
Wisdom with Time

From *The Green Helmet and Other Poems* (1912)

Though leaves are many, the root is one;
Through all the lying days of my youth
I swayed my leaves and flowers in the sun;
Now I may wither into the truth.

A Lyric from an Unpublished Play

From *The Green Helmet and Other Poems* (1912)
Later entitled 'The Mask'

'Put off that mask of burning gold
With emerald eyes.'
'O no, my dear, you make so bold
To find if hearts be wild and wise,
And yet not cold.'

'I would but find what's there to find,
Love or deceit.'
'It was the mask engaged your mind,
And after set your heart to beat,
Not what's behind.'

'But lest you are my enemy,
I must enquire.'
'O no, my dear, let all that be,
What matter, so there is but fire
In you, in me?'

At the Abbey Theatre
(Imitated from Ronsard)

From *The Green Helmet and Other Poems* (1912)

Dear Craoibhin Aoibhin, look into our case.
When we are high and airy hundreds say
That if we hold that flight they'll leave the place,
While those same hundreds mock another day
Because we have made our art of common things,
So bitterly, you'd dream they longed to look
All their lives through into some drift of wings.
You've dandled them and fed them from the book
And know them to the bone; impart to us—
We'll keep the secret—a new trick to please.
Is there a bridle for this Proteus
That turns and changes like his draughty seas?
Or is there none, most popular of men,
But when they mock us that we mock again?

At Galway Races

From *The Green Helmet and Other Poems* (1912)

Out yonder, where the racecourse is,
Delight makes all of the one mind,
Riders upon the swift horses,
The field that closes in behind:
We, too, had good attendance once,
Hearers and hearteners of the work;
Aye, horsemen for companions,
Before the merchant and the clerk
Breathed on the world with timid breath.
Sing on: sometime, and at some new moon,
We'll learn that sleeping is not death,
Hearing the whole earth change its tune,
Its flesh being wild, and it again
Crying aloud as the racecourse is,
And we find hearteners among men
That ride upon horses.

All Things can tempt Me

From *The Green Helmet and Other Poems* (1912)

All things can tempt me from this craft of verse:
One time it was a woman's face, or worse—
The seeming needs of my fool-driven land;
Now nothing but comes readier to the hand
Than this accustomed toil. When I was young,
I had not given a penny for a song
Did not the poet sing it with such airs
That one believed he had a sword upstairs;
Yet would be now, could I but have my wish,
Colder and dumber and deafer than a fish.

The Young Man's Song

From *The Green Helmet and Other Poems* (1912)
Later entitled 'Brown Penny'

I whispered, 'I am too young,'
And then, 'I am old enough,'
Wherefore I threw a penny
To find out if I might love;
'Go and love, go and love, young man,
If the lady be young and fair,'
Ah, penny, brown penny, brown penny,
I am looped in the loops of her hair.

Oh love is the crooked thing,
There is nobody wise enough
To find out all that is in it,
For he would be thinking of love
Till the stars had run away,
And the shadows eaten the moon;
Ah, penny, brown penny, brown penny,
One cannot begin it too soon.

September 1913

From *Responsibilities* (1914)

What need you, being come to sense,
But fumble in a greasy till
And add the halfpence to the pence
And prayer to shivering prayer, until
You have dried the marrow from the bone?
For men were born to pray and save:
Romantic Ireland's dead and gone,
It's with O'Leary in the grave.

Yet they were of a different kind,
The names that stilled your childish play,
They have gone about the world like wind,
But little time had they to pray
For whom the hangman's rope was spun,
And what, God help us, could they save?
Romantic Ireland's dead and gone,
It's with O'Leary in the grave.

Was it for this the wild geese spread
The grey wing upon every tide;
For this that all that blood was shed,

For this Edward Fitzgerald died,
And Robert Emmet and Wolfe Tone,
All that delirium of the brave;
Romantic Ireland's dead and gone,
It's with O'Leary in the grave.

Yet could we turn the years again,
And call those exiles as they were,
In all their loneliness and pain
You'd cry, 'Some woman's yellow hair
Has maddened every mother's son':
They weighed so lightly what they gave,
But let them be, they're dead and gone,
They're with O'Leary in the grave.

To a Shade

From *Responsibilities* (1914)

If you have revisited the town, thin Shade,
Whether to look upon your monument
(I wonder if the builder has been paid)
Or happier thoughted when the day is spent
To drink of that salt breath out of the sea
When grey gulls flit about instead of men,
And the gaunt houses put on majesty:
Let these content you and be gone again;
For they are at their old tricks yet.

                        A man
Of your own passionate serving kind who had
    brought
In his full hands what, had they only known,
Had given their children's children loftier thought,
Sweeter emotion, working in their veins
Like gentle blood, has been driven from the place,
And insult heaped upon him for his pains
And for his open-handedness, disgrace;
Your enemy, an old foul mouth, had set
The pack upon him.

                 Go, unquiet wanderer,

And gather the Glasnevin coverlet
About your head till the dust stops your ear,
The time for you to taste of that salt breath
And listen at the corners has not come;
You had enough of sorrow before death—
Away, away! You are safer in the tomb.

September 29, 1913

When Helen Lived

From *Responsibilities* (1914)

We have cried in our despair
That men desert,
For some trivial affair
Or noisy, insolent sport,
Beauty that we have won
From bitterest hours;
Yet we, had we walked within
Those topless towers
Where Helen walked with her boy,
Had given but as the rest
Of the men and women of Troy,
A word and a jest.

A Memory of Youth

From *Responsibilities* (1914)

The moments passed as at a play,
I had the wisdom love brings forth;
I had my share of mother-wit
And yet for all that I could say,
And though I had her praise for it,
A cloud blown from the cut-throat North
Suddenly hid Love's moon away.

Believing every word I said,
I praised her body and her mind
Till pride had made her eyes grow bright,
And pleasure made her cheeks grow red,
And vanity her footfall light,
Yet we, for all that praise, could find
Nothing but darkness overhead.

We sat as silent as a stone,
We knew, though she'd not said a word,
That even the best of love must die,
And had been savagely undone

Were it not that Love upon the cry
Of a most ridiculous little bird
Tore from the clouds his marvellous moon.

Fallen Majesty

From *Responsibilities* (1914)

Although crowds gathered once if she but showed
    her face,
And even old men's eyes grew dim, this hand alone,
Like some last courtier at a gypsy camping place,
Babbling of fallen majesty, records what's gone.

The lineaments, a heart that laughter has made
    sweet,
These, these remain, but I record what's gone. A
    crowd
Will gather, and not know it walks the very street
Whereon a thing once walked that seemed a
    burning cloud.

An Appointment

From *Responsibilities* (1914)

Being out of heart with government
I took a broken root to fling
Where the proud, wayward squirrel went,
Taking delight that he could spring;
And he, with that low whinnying sound
That is like laughter, sprang again
And so to the other tree at a bound.
Nor the tame will, nor timid brain,
Nor heavy knitting of the brow
Bred that fierce tooth and cleanly limb
And threw him up to laugh on the bough;
No government appointed him.

A Coat

From *Responsibilities* (1914)

I made my song a coat
Covered with embroideries
Out of old mythologies
From heel to throat;
But the fools caught it,
Wore it in the world's eye
As though they'd wrought it.
Song, let them take it,
For there's more enterprise
In walking naked.

While I, from that reed-throated whisperer
Who comes at need, although not now as once
A clear articulation in the air
But inwardly, surmise companions
Beyond the fling of the dull ass's hoof,
—Ben Jonson's phrase—and find when June is come
At Kyle-na-no under that ancient roof

A sterner conscience and a friendlier home,
I can forgive even that wrong of wrongs,
Those undreamt accidents that have made me
—Seeing that Fame has perished this long while,
Being but a part of ancient ceremony—
Notorious, till all my priceless things
Are but a post the passing dogs defile.

The Wild Swans at Coole

From *The Wild Swans at Coole* (1919)

The trees are in their autumn beauty,
The woodland paths are dry,
Under the October twilight the water
Mirrors a still sky;
Upon the brimming water among the stones
Are nine-and-fifty swans.

The nineteenth autumn has come upon me
Since I first made my count;
I saw, before I had well finished,
All suddenly mount
And scatter wheeling in great broken rings
Upon their clamorous wings.

I have looked upon those brilliant creatures,
And now my heart is sore.
All's changed since I, hearing at twilight,
The first time on this shore,
The bell-beat of their wings above my head,
Trod with a lighter tread.
Unwearied still, lover by lover,

They paddle in the cold,
Companionable streams or climb the air;
Their hearts have not grown old;
Passion or conquest, wander where they will,
Attend upon them still.
But now they drift on the still water
Mysterious, beautiful;
Among what rushes will they build,
By what lake's edge or pool
Delight men's eyes, when I awake some day
To find they have flown away?

In Memory of
Major Robert Gregory

From *The Wild Swans at Coole* (1919)

I

Now that we're almost settled in our house
I'll name the friends that cannot sup with us
Beside a fire of turf in the ancient tower,
And having talked to some late hour
Climb up the narrow winding stair to bed:
Discoverers of forgotten truth
Or mere companions of my youth,
All, all are in my thoughts to-night, being dead.

II

Always we'd have the new friend meet the old,
And we are hurt if either friend seem cold,
And there is salt to lengthen out the smart
In the affections of our heart,
And quarrels are blown up upon that head;
But not a friend that I would bring

This night can set us quarrelling,
For all that come into my mind are dead.

III

Lionel Johnson comes the first to mind,
That loved his learning better than mankind,
Though courteous to the worst; much falling he
Brooded upon sanctity
Till all his Greek and Latin learning seemed
A long blast upon the horn that brought
A little nearer to his thought
A measureless consummation that he dreamed.

IV

And that enquiring man John Synge comes next,
That dying chose the living world for text
And never could have rested in the tomb
But that, long travelling, he had come
Towards nightfall upon certain set apart
In a most desolate stony place,
Towards nightfall upon a race
Passionate and simple like his heart.

V

And then I think of old George Pollexfen,
In muscular youth well known to Mayo men
For horsemanship at meets or at racecourses,
That could have shown how pure-bred horses
And solid men, for all their passion, live

But as the outrageous stars incline
By opposition, square and trine;
Having grown sluggish and contemplative.

VI

They were my close companions many a year,
A portion of my mind and life, as it were,
And now their breathless faces seem to look
Out of some old picture-book;
I am accustomed to their lack of breath,
But not that my dear friend's dear son,
Our Sidney and our perfect man,
Could share in that discourtesy of death.

VII

For all things the delighted eye now sees
Were loved by him; the old storm-broken trees
That cast their shadows upon road and bridge;
The tower set on the stream's edge;
The ford where drinking cattle make a stir
Nightly, and startled by that sound
The water-hen must change her ground;
He might have been your heartiest welcomer.

VIII

When with the Galway foxhounds he would ride
From Castle Taylor to the Roxborough side
Or Esserkelly plain, few kept his pace;
At Mooneen he had leaped a place

So perilous that half the astonished meet
Had shut their eyes, and where was it
He rode a race without a bit?
And yet his mind outran the horses' feet.

IX

We dreamed that a great painter had been born
To cold Clare rock and Galway rock and thorn,
To that stern colour and that delicate line
That are our secret discipline
Wherein the gazing heart doubles her might.
Soldier, scholar, horseman, he,
And yet he had the intensity
To have published all to be a world's delight.

X

What other could so well have counselled us
In all lovely intricacies of a house
As he that practised or that understood
All work in metal or in wood,
In moulded plaster or in carven stone?
Soldier, scholar, horseman, he,
And all he did done perfectly
As though he had but that one trade alone.

XI

Some burn damp fagots, others may consume
The entire combustible world in one small room
As though dried straw, and if we turn about

The bare chimney is gone black out
Because the work had finished in that flare.
Soldier, scholar, horseman, he,
As 'twere all life's epitome.
What made us dream that he could comb grey hair?

XII

I had thought, seeing how bitter is that wind
That shakes the shutter, to have brought to mind
All those that manhood tried, or childhood loved,
Or boyish intellect approved,
With some appropriate commentary on each;
Until imagination brought
A fitter welcome; but a thought
Of that late death took all my heart for speech.

An Irish Airman
foresees his Death

Composed 1918
From *The Wild Swans at Coole* (1919)

I know that I shall meet my fate
Somewhere among the clouds above;
Those that I fight I do not hate,
Those that I guard I do not love;
My country is Kiltartan Cross,
My countrymen Kiltartan's poor,
No likely end could bring them loss
Or leave them happier than before.
Nor law, nor duty bade me fight,
Nor public man, nor cheering crowds,
A lonely impulse of delight
Drove to this tumult in the clouds;
I balanced all, brought all to mind,
The years to come seemed waste of breath,
A waste of breath the years behind
In balance with this life, this death.

Men improve with the Years

From *The Wild Swans at Coole* (1919)

I am worn out with dreams;
A weather-worn, marble triton
Among the streams;
And all day long I look
Upon this lady's beauty
As though I had found in book
A pictured beauty,
Pleased to have filled the eyes
Or the discerning ears,
Delighted to be but wise,
For men improve with the years;
And yet, and yet,
Is this my dream, or the truth?
O would that we had met When I had my
burning youth;
But I grow old among dreams,
A weather-worn, marble triton
Among the streams.

Solomon to Sheba

From *The Wild Swans at Coole* (1919)

Sang Solomon to Sheba,
And kissed her dusky face,
'All day long from mid-day
We have talked in the one place,
All day long from shadowless noon
We have gone round and round
In the narrow theme of love
Like an old horse in a pound.'

To Solomon sang Sheba,
Planted on his knees,
'If you had broached a matter
That might the learned please,
You had before the sun had thrown
Our shadows on the ground
Discovered that my thoughts, not it,
Are but a narrow pound.'

Sang Solomon to Sheba,
And kissed her Arab eyes,
'There's not a man or woman

Born under the skies
Dare match in learning with us two,
And all day long we have found
There's not a thing but love can make
The world a narrow pound.'

The Living Beauty

From *The Wild Swans at Coole* (1919)

I bade, because the wick and oil are spent
And frozen are the channels of the blood,
My discontented heart to draw content
From beauty that is cast out of a mould
In bronze, or that in dazzling marble appears,
Appears, but when we have gone is gone again,
Being more indifferent to our solitude
Than 'twere an apparition. O heart, we are old;
The living beauty is for younger men:
We cannot pay its tribute of wild tears.

A Song

From *The Wild Swans at Coole* (1919)

I thought no more was needed
Youth to prolong
Than dumb-bell and foil
To keep the body young.
O who could have foretold
That the heart grows old?

Though I have many words,
What woman's satisfied,
I am no longer faint
Because at her side?
O who could have foretold
That the heart grows old?

I have not lost desire
But the heart that I had;
I thought 'twould burn my body
Laid on the death-bed,
For who could have foretold
That the heart grows old?

Lines written in Dejection

From *The Wild Swans at Coole* (1919)

When have I last looked on
The round green eyes and the long wavering bodies
Of the dark leopards of the moon?
All the wild witches, those most noble ladies,
For all their broom-sticks and their tears,
Their angry tears, are gone.
The holy centaurs of the hills are vanished;
I have nothing but the embittered sun;
Banished heroic mother moon and vanished,
And now that I have come to fifty years
I must endure the timid sun.

The Dawn

From *The Wild Swans at Coole* (1919)

I would be ignorant as the dawn
That has looked down
On that old queen measuring a town
With the pin of a brooch,
Or on the withered men that saw
From their pedantic Babylon
The careless planets in their courses,
The stars fade out where the moon comes,
And took their tablets and did sums;
I would be ignorant as the dawn
That merely stood, rocking the glittering coach
Above the cloudy shoulders of the horses;
I would be—for no knowledge is worth a straw—
Ignorant and wanton as the dawn.

On Woman

From *The Wild Swans at Coole* (1919)

May God be praised for woman
That gives up all her mind,
A man may find in no man
A friendship of her kind
That covers all he has brought
As with her flesh and bone,
Nor quarrels with a thought
Because it is not her own.

Though pedantry denies
It's plain the Bible means
That Solomon grew wise
While talking with his queens.
Yet never could, although
They say he counted grass,
Count all the praises due
When Sheba was his lass,
When she the iron wrought, or
When from the smithy fire
It shuddered in the water:
Harshness of their desire

That made them stretch and yawn,
Pleasure that comes with sleep,
Shudder that made them one.
What else He give or keep
God grant me—no, not here,
For I am not so bold
To hope a thing so dear
Now I am growing old,
But when if the tale's true
The Pestle of the moon
That pounds up all anew
Brings me to birth again—
To find what once I had
And know what once I have known,
Until I am driven mad,
Sleep driven from my bed,
By tenderness and care,
Pity, an aching head,
Gnashing of teeth, despair;
And all because of some one
Perverse creature of chance,
And live like Solomon
That Sheba led a dance.

The Fisherman

From *The Wild Swans at Coole* (1919)

Although I can see him still,
The freckled man who goes
To a grey place on a hill
In grey Connemara clothes
At dawn to cast his flies,
It's long since I began
To call up to the eyes
This wise and simple man.
All day I'd looked in the face
What I had hoped 'twould be
To write for my own race
And the reality;
The living men that I hate,
The dead man that I loved,
The craven man in his seat,
The insolent unreproved,
And no knave brought to book
Who has won a drunken cheer,
The witty man and his joke
Aimed at the commonest ear,
The clever man who cries

The catch-cries of the clown,
The beating down of the wise
And great Art beaten down.

Maybe a twelvemonth since
Suddenly I began,
In scorn of this audience,
Imagining a man,
And his sun-freckled face,
And grey Connemara cloth,
Climbing up to a place
Where stone is dark under froth,
And the down-turn of his wrist
When the flies drop in the stream;
A man who does not exist,
A man who is but a dream;
And cried, 'Before I am old
I shall have written him one
Poem maybe as cold
And passionate as the dawn.'

Her Praise

From *The Wild Swans at Coole* (1919)

She is foremost of those that I would hear praised.
I have gone about the house, gone up and down
As a man does who has published a new book
Or a young girl dressed out in her new gown,
And though I have turned the talk by hook or crook
Until her praise should be the uppermost theme,
A woman spoke of some new tale she had read,
A man confusedly in a half dream
As though some other name ran in his head.
She is foremost of those that I would hear praised.
I will talk no more of books or the long war
But walk by the dry thorn until I have found
Some beggar sheltering from the wind, and there
Manage the talk until her name come round.
If there be rags enough he will know her name
And be well pleased remembering it, for in the old
    days,
Though she had young men's praise and old men's
    blame,
Among the poor both old and young gave her
    praise.

Broken Dreams

From *The Wild Swans at Coole* (1919)

There is grey in your hair.
Young men no longer suddenly catch their breath
When you are passing;
But maybe some old gaffer mutters a blessing
Because it was your prayer
Recovered him upon the bed of death.
For your sole sake—that all heart's ache have
    known,
And given to others all heart's ache,
From meagre girlhood's putting on
Burdensome beauty—for your sole sake
Heaven has put away the stroke of her doom,
So great her portion in that peace you make
By merely walking in a room.

Your beauty can but leave among us
Vague memories, nothing but memories.
A young man when the old men are done talking
Will say to an old man, 'Tell me of that lady
The poet stubborn with his passion sang us
When age might well have chilled his blood.'

Vague memories, nothing but memories,
But in the grave all, all, shall be renewed.
The certainty that I shall see that lady
Leaning or standing or walking
In the first loveliness of womanhood,
And with the fervour of my youthful eyes,
Has set me muttering like a fool.

You are more beautiful than any one
And yet your body had a flaw:
Your small hands were not beautiful,
And I am afraid that you will run
And paddle to the wrist
In that mysterious, always brimming lake
Where those that have obeyed the holy law
Paddle and are perfect. Leave unchanged
The hands that I have kissed
For old sakes' sake.

The last stroke of midnight dies.
All day in the one chair
From dream to dream and rhyme to rhyme I have
    ranged
In rambling talk with an image of air:
Vague memories, nothing but memories.

On being asked for a War Poem

From *The Wild Swans at Coole* (1919)

I think it better that in times like these
A poet keep his mouth shut, for in truth
We have no gift to set a statesman right;
He has had enough of meddling who can please
A young girl in the indolence of her youth,
Or an old man upon a winter's night.

Two Songs of a Fool

From *The Wild Swans at Coole* (1919)

I

A speckled cat and a tame hare
Eat at my hearthstone
And sleep there;
And both look up to me alone
For learning and defence
As I look up to Providence.

I start out of my sleep to think
Some day I may forget
Their food and drink;
Or, the house door left unshut,
The hare may run till it's found
The horn's sweet note and the tooth of the hound.

I bear a burden that might well try
Men that do all by rule,
And what can I
That am a wandering-witted fool

But pray to God that He ease
My great responsibilities.

II

I slept on my three-legged stool by the fire,
The speckled cat slept on my knee;
We never thought to enquire
Where the brown hare might be,
And whether the door were shut.
Who knows how she drank the wind
Stretched up on two legs from the mat,
Before she had settled her mind
To drum with her heel and to leap:
Had I but awakened from sleep
And called her name she had heard,
It may be, and had not stirred,
That now, it may be, has found
The horn's sweet note and the tooth of the hound.

Michael Robartes and
The Dancer

From *Michael Robartes and the Dancer* (1921)

HE

Opinion is not worth a rush;
In this altar-piece the knight,
Who grips his long spear so to push
That dragon through the fading light,
Loved the lady; and it's plain
The half-dead dragon was her thought,
That every morning rose again
And dug its claws and shrieked and fought.
Could the impossible come to pass
She would have time to turn her eyes,
Her lover thought, upon the glass
And on the instant would grow wise.

SHE

You mean they argued.

HE

Put it so;
But bear in mind your lover's wage
Is what your looking-glass can show,
And that he will turn green with rage
At all that is not pictured there.

SHE

May I not put myself to college?
HE. Go pluck Athena by the hair;
For what mere book can grant a knowledge
With an impassioned gravity
Appropriate to that beating breast,
That vigorous thigh, that dreaming eye?
And may the devil take the rest.

SHE

And must no beautiful woman be
Learned like a man?

HE

Paul Veronese
And all his sacred company
Imagined bodies all their days
By the lagoon you love so much,
For proud, soft, ceremonious proof
That all must come to sight and touch;
While Michael Angelo's Sistine roof
His 'Morning' and his 'Night' disclose
How sinew that has been pulled tight,
Or it may be loosened in repose,

Can rule by supernatural right
Yet be but sinew.

SHE

I have heard said
There is great danger in the body.
HE
Did God in portioning wine and bread
Give man His thought or His mere body?

SHE

My wretched dragon is perplexed.

HE

I have principles to prove me right.
It follows from this Latin text
That blest souls are not composite,
And that all beautiful women may
Live in uncomposite blessedness,
And lead us to the like—if they
Will banish every thought, unless
The lineaments that please their view
When the long looking-glass is full,
Even from the foot-sole think it too.

SHE

They say such different things at school.

Solomon and the Witch

From *Michael Robartes and the Dancer* (1921)

And thus declared that Arab lady:
'Last night, where under the wild moon
On grassy mattress I had laid me,
Within my arms great Solomon,
I suddenly cried out in a strange tongue
Not his, not mine.'
            Who understood
Whatever has been said, sighed, sung,
Howled, miau-d, barked, brayed, belled, yelled,
    cried, crowed,
Thereon replied: 'A cockerel
Crew from a blossoming apple bough
Three hundred years before the Fall,
And never crew again till now,
And would not now but that he thought,
Chance being at one with Choice at last,
All that the brigand apple brought
And this foul world were dead at last.
He that crowed out eternity
Thought to have crowed it in again.
For though love has a spider's eye

To find out some appropriate pain—
Aye, though all passion's in the glance—
For every nerve, and tests a lover
With cruelties of Choice and Chance;
And when at last that murder's over
Maybe the bride-bed brings despair,
For each an imagined image brings
And finds a real image there;
Yet the world ends when these two things,
Though several, are a single light,
When oil and wick are burned in one;
Therefore a blessed moon last night
Gave Sheba to her Solomon.'

'Yet the world stays':
                                    'If that be so,
Your cockerel found us in the wrong
Although he thought it worth a crow.
Maybe an image is too strong
Or maybe is not strong enough.'

'The night has fallen; not a sound
In the forbidden sacred grove
Unless a petal hit the ground,
Nor any human sight within it
But the crushed grass where we have lain;
And the moon is wilder every minute.
O! Solomon! let us try again.'

An Image from a Past Life

From *Michael Robartes and the Dancer* (1921)

He

Never until this night have I been stirred.
The elaborate star-light has thrown reflections
On the dark stream,
Till all the eddies gleam;
And thereupon there comes that scream
From terrified, invisible beast or bird:
Image of poignant recollection.

She

An image of my heart that is smitten through
Out of all likelihood, or reason,
And when at last,
Youth's bitterness being past,
I had thought that all my days were cast
Amid most lovely places; smitten as though
It had not learned its lesson.

He

Why have you laid your hands upon my eyes?
What can have suddenly alarmed you

Whereon 'twere best
My eyes should never rest?
What is there but the slowly fading west,
The river imaging the flashing skies,
All that to this moment charmed you?

SHE

A sweetheart from another life floats there
As though she had been forced to linger
From vague distress
Or arrogant loveliness,
Merely to loosen out a tress
Among the starry eddies of her hair
Upon the paleness of a finger.

HE

But why should you grow suddenly afraid
And start—I at your shoulder—
Imagining
That any night could bring
An image up, or anything
Even to eyes that beauty had driven mad,
But images to make me fonder.

SHE

Now she has thrown her arms above her head;
Whether she threw them up to flout me,
Or but to find,
Now that no fingers bind,
That her hair streams upon the wind,
I do not know, that know I am afraid
Of the hovering thing night brought me.

Easter 1916

From *Michael Robartes and the Dancer* (1921)

I have met them at close of day
Coming with vivid faces
From counter or desk among grey
Eighteenth-century houses.
I have passed with a nod of the head
Or polite meaningless words,
Or have lingered awhile and said
Polite meaningless words,
And thought before I had done
Of a mocking tale or a gibe
To please a companion
Around the fire at the club,
Being certain that they and I
But lived where motley is worn:
All changed, changed utterly:
A terrible beauty is born.

That woman's days were spent
In ignorant good will,
Her nights in argument
Until her voice grew shrill.

What voice more sweet than hers
When young and beautiful,
She rode to harriers?
This man had kept a school
And rode our winged horse.
This other his helper and friend
Was coming into his force;
He might have won fame in the end,
So sensitive his nature seemed,
So daring and sweet his thought.
This other man I had dreamed
A drunken, vainglorious lout.
He had done most bitter wrong
To some who are near my heart,
Yet I number him in the song;
He, too, has resigned his part
In the casual comedy;
He, too, has been changed in his turn,
Transformed utterly:
A terrible beauty is born.

Hearts with one purpose alone
Through summer and winter seem
Enchanted to a stone
To trouble the living stream.
The horse that comes from the road.
The rider, the birds that range
From cloud to tumbling cloud,
Minute by minute change;
A shadow of cloud on the stream
Changes minute by minute;
A horse-hoof slides on the brim,

And a horse plashes within it
Where long-legged moor-hens dive,
And hens to moor-cocks call.
Minute by minute they live:
The stone's in the midst of all.

Too long a sacrifice
Can make a stone of the heart.
O when may it suffice?
That is heaven's part, our part
To murmur name upon name,
As a mother names her child
When sleep at last has come
On limbs that had run wild.
What is it but nightfall?
No, no, not night but death;
Was it needless death after all?
For England may keep faith
For all that is done and said.
We know their dream; enough
To know they dreamed and are dead.
And what if excess of love
Bewildered them till they died?
I write it out in a verse—
MacDonagh and MacBride
And Connolly and Pearse
Now and in time to be,
Wherever green is worn,
Are changed, changed utterly:
A terrible beauty is born.

September 25, 1916

Sixteen Dead Men

From *Michael Robartes and the Dancer* (1921)

O but we talked at large before
The sixteen men were shot,
But who can talk of give and take,
What should be and what not
While those dead men are loitering there
To stir the boiling pot?

You say that we should still the land
Till Germany's overcome;
But who is there to argue that
Now Pearse is deaf and dumb?
And is their logic to outweigh
MacDonagh's bony thumb?

How could you dream they'd listen
That have an ear alone
For those new comrades they have found
Lord Edward and Wolfe Tone,
Or meddle with our give and take
That converse bone to bone.

The Rose Tree

From *Michael Robartes and the Dancer* (1921)

'O words are lightly spoken'
Said Pearse to Connolly,
'Maybe a breath of politic words
Has withered our Rose Tree;
Or maybe but a wind that blows
Across the bitter sea.'

'It needs to be but watered,'
James Connolly replied,
'To make the green come out again
And spread on every side,
And shake the blossom from the bud
To be the garden's pride.'

'But where can we draw water,'
Said Pearse to Connolly,
'When all the wells are parched away?
O plain as plain can be
There's nothing but our own red blood
Can make a right Rose Tree.'

On a Political Prisoner

From *Michael Robartes and the Dancer* (1921)

She that but little patience knew,
From childhood on, had now so much
A grey gull lost its fear and flew
Down to her cell and there alit,
And there endured her fingers' touch
And from her fingers ate its bit.

Did she in touching that lone wing
Recall the years before her mind
Became a bitter, an abstract thing,
Her thought some popular enmity:
Blind and leader of the blind
Drinking the foul ditch where they lie?

When long ago I saw her ride
Under Ben Bulben to the meet,
The beauty of her country-side
With all youth's lonely wildness stirred,
She seemed to have grown clean and sweet
Like any rock-bred, sea-borne bird:
Sea-borne, or balanced on the air

When first it sprang out of the nest
Upon some lofty rock to stare
Upon the cloudy canopy,
While under its storm-beaten breast
Cried out the hollows of the sea.

Demon and Beast

From *Michael Robartes and the Dancer* (1921)

For certain minutes at the least
That crafty demon and that loud beast
That plague me day and night
Ran out of my sight;
Though I had long perned in the gyre,
Between my hatred and desire,
I saw my freedom won
And all laugh in the sun.

The glittering eyes in a death's head
Of old Luke Wadding's portrait said
Welcome, and the Ormondes all
Nodded upon the wall,
And even Stafford smiled as though
It made him happier to know
I understood his plan;
Now that the loud beast ran
There was no portrait in the Gallery
But beckoned to sweet company,
For all men's thoughts grew clear
Being dear as mine are dear.

But soon a tear-drop started up
For aimless joy had made me stop
Beside the little lake
To watch a white gull take
A bit of bread thrown up into the air;
Now gyring down and perning there
He splashed where an absurd
Portly green-pated bird
Shook off the water from his back;
Being no more demoniac
A stupid happy creature
Could rouse my whole nature.

Yet I am certain as can be
That every natural victory
Belongs to beast or demon,
That never yet had freeman
Right mastery of natural things,
And that mere growing old, that brings
Chilled blood, this sweetness brought;
Yet have no dearer thought
Than that I may find out a way
To make it linger half a day.

O what a sweetness strayed
Through barren Thebaid,
Or by the Mareotic sea
When that exultant Anthony
And twice a thousand more
Starved upon the shore
And withered to a bag of bones:
What had the Caesars but their thrones?

The Second Coming

From *Michael Robartes and the Dancer* (1921)

Turning and turning in the widening gyre
The falcon cannot hear the falconer;
Things fall apart; the centre cannot hold;
Mere anarchy is loosed upon the world,
The blood-dimmed tide is loosed, and everywhere
The ceremony of innocence is drowned;
The best lack all conviction, while the worst
Are full of passionate intensity.

Surely some revelation is at hand;
Surely the Second Coming is at hand.
The Second Coming! Hardly are those words out
When a vast image out of *Spiritus Mundi*
Troubles my sight: somewhere in the sands of desert
A shape with lion body and the head of a man,
A gaze blank and pitiless as the sun,
Is moving its slow thighs, while all about it
Reel shadows of the indignant desert birds.
The darkness drops again; but now I know
That twenty centuries of stony sleep

Were vexed to nightmare by a rocking cradle,
And what rough beast, its hour come round at last,
Slouches towards Bethlehem to be born?

A Prayer for my Daughter

From *Michael Robartes and the Dancer* (1921)

Once more the storm is howling and half hid
Under this cradle-hood and coverlid
My child sleeps on. There is no obstacle
But Gregory's Wood and one bare hill
Whereby the haystack- and roof-levelling wind,
Bred on the Atlantic, can be stayed;
And for an hour I have walked and prayed
Because of the great gloom that is in my mind.

I have walked and prayed for this young child
    an hour
And heard the sea-wind scream upon the tower,
And under the arches of the bridge, and scream
In the elms above the flooded stream;
Imagining in excited reverie
That the future years had come,
Dancing to a frenzied drum,
Out of the murderous innocence of the sea.

May she be granted beauty and yet not
Beauty to make a stranger's eye distraught,
Or hers before a looking-glass, for such,
Being made beautiful overmuch,
Consider beauty a sufficient end,
Lose natural kindness and maybe
The heart-revealing intimacy
That chooses right and never find a friend.

Helen being chosen found life flat and dull
And later had much trouble from a fool,
While that great Queen, that rose out of the spray,
Being fatherless could have her way
Yet chose a bandy-legged smith for man.
It's certain that fine women eat
A crazy salad with their meat
Whereby the Horn of Plenty is undone.

In courtesy I'd have her chiefly learned;
Hearts are not had as a gift but hearts are earned
By those that are not entirely beautiful;
Yet many, that have played the fool
For beauty's very self, has charm made wise,
And many a poor man that has roved,
Loved and thought himself beloved,
From a glad kindness cannot take his eyes.

May she become a flourishing hidden tree
That all her thoughts may like the linnet be,
And have no business but dispensing round
Their magnanimities of sound,

Nor but in merriment begin a chase,
Nor but in merriment a quarrel.
O may she live like some green laurel
Rooted in one dear perpetual place.

My mind, because the minds that I have loved,
The sort of beauty that I have approved,
Prosper but little, has dried up of late,
Yet knows that to be choked with hate
May well be of all evil chances chief.
If there's no hatred in a mind
Assault and battery of the wind
Can never tear the linnet from the leaf.

An intellectual hatred is the worst,
So let her think opinions are accursed.
Have I not seen the loveliest woman born
Out of the mouth of Plenty's horn,
Because of her opinionated mind
Barter that horn and every good
By quiet natures understood
For an old bellows full of angry wind?

Considering that, all hatred driven hence,
The soul recovers radical innocence
And learns at last that it is self-delighting,
Self-appeasing, self-affrighting,
And that its own sweet will is Heaven's will;
She can, though every face should scowl
And every windy quarter howl
Or every bellows burst, be happy still.

And may her bride-groom bring her to a house
Where all's accustomed, ceremonious;
For arrogance and hatred are the wares
Peddled in the thoroughfares.
How but in custom and in ceremony
Are innocence and beauty born?
Ceremony's a name for the rich horn,
And custom for the spreading laurel tree.

June 1919

A Meditation in Time of War

From *Michael Robartes and the Dancer* (1921)

For one throb of the Artery,
While on that old grey stone I sat
Under the old wind-broken tree,
I knew that One is animate
Mankind inanimate fantasy.

To be carved on a Stone at Ballylee

From *Michael Robartes and the Dancer* (1921)

I, the poet William Yeats,
With old mill boards and sea-green slates,
And smithy work from the Gort forge,
Restored this tower for my wife George;
And may these characters remain
When all is ruin once again.

Index of Titles